PERDITION

A Scottish murder mystery with a shocking twist

PETE BRASSETT

THE
BOOK
FOLKS

Paperback published by The Book Folks

London, 2018

ISBN 978-1-9833-5392-5

www.thebookfolks.com

PERDITION is the seventh novel by Pete Brassett to feature detectives Munro and West. Look out for SHE, the first book, and AVARICE, ENMITY, DUPLICITY, TERMINUS and TALION. All of these books can be enjoyed on their own, or as a series.

Prologue

Often described as an affable and somewhat altruistic individual, James Munro – on the cusp of retirement after nearly forty years of active service – was willing to tolerate most things in life apart from cyclists who deemed themselves exempt from the regulations of the Highway Code; those who consumed fetid fast food on public transport; and the ear-splitting screech of a chop saw as the team of carpenters who'd arrived at 6 a.m. set about replacing the fire-damaged roof timbers, joists and floorboards in the kitchen and guest bedroom to the rear of his house.

Alone in the lounge with his patience wearing thin, he took a deep breath, ran his fingers through his thinning, grey hair and – wary he'd be held responsible for the village's first ever sugar shortage as a result of repeated requests for mugs of sweet tea – reached for his coat, tucked two bars of Kendal Mint Cake into his pocket, and headed for Criffel where, despite the light cloud, the unfettered view from the summit towards the Lake District was as rewarding as ever.

Saddled with the prospect of sharing his house with a battalion of builders for the foreseeable future and with it, the unavoidable disruption to his daily routine, he contemplated returning to Skye for a relaxing break before deciding on the much shorter, and altogether less taxing trip to Ayr where, upon retrieving his belongings from the office, he would, somewhat reluctantly, discuss the topic of his imminent retirement with DCI George Elliot.

* * *

Resigned to the fact that Munro's long-awaited departure was now in the bag, leaving her without the safety net she'd come to rely upon, a sullen-faced West – looking more like a cat burglar in her tight, black polo-neck and matching jeans than a salaried police officer – pinned her tumbling locks atop her head and pulled up a chair, the initial findings of the post-mortem in one hand, and a double-bacon buttie in the other.

'Have you read this?' she said, wiping a dollop of brown sauce from her lips.

'Aye, miss,' said Dougal as he sifted through the victim's belongings, 'If only every case we had was as clean-cut as this.'

'How d'you mean?'

'Well, it's not often we get a body carrying full ID and a conclusive cause of death from the pathologist. It's like buying a present for someone and finding out that the batteries are actually included.'

'Yeah, I suppose so,' said West. 'You got anything interesting there?'

'Nothing out of the ordinary. A wallet with a bundle of notes, an Omega wristwatch, a string of beads, keys, and a mobile phone.'

'Have next of kin been informed?'

'Aye, so far as I know.'

'Good,' said West, polishing off her roll, 'all we have to do now is figure out if it was suicide or if somebody topped him.'

Duncan put down his newspaper, scratched the stubble on his chin, and made for the kettle.

'Sounds like misadventure to me,' he said.

'Your life's one big misadventure,' said West with a smile. 'Sorry boys but I just can't see this johnny killing himself, not like this.'

'That's why I'm saying, misadventure.'

'Go on, then. Explain.'

'Okay,' said Duncan. 'The report says his body was loaded with a lethal dose of Buprenorphine, right?'

'If you say so.'

'And Buprenorphine's used for pain relief. Not a wee headache or anything like that, I'm talking extreme, chronic pain. Like cancer.'

'But he didn't have cancer.'

'No,' said Dougal, 'he didn't, but that's not all it's used for. It's an opioid. They use it for weaning addicts off the hard stuff, too, you know, like heroin, for example.'

West, her interest roused, stared at Dougal inquisitively.

'You mean, kind of like methadone?'

'Aye, exactly.'

'So, you reckon if he was a user, he could've got his hands on this stuff and what? Just overdosed?'

'Aye, why not?' said Duncan as he handed out the tea. 'The only problem is, with so much of the stuff in his body, the pathologist can't be certain if he was using or not. Not yet, anyway.'

'Well, that's a great help,' said West with a sigh, 'but you're already assuming he took the stuff himself.'

'I am,' said Duncan. 'Let's face it, miss, if somebody had killed him, then why waste money on expensive drugs when there's cheaper ways of doing it. Besides, Buprenorphine's not the kind of thing you'd pick up on the street.'

'So, you're saying it's not easy to come by, then?'

'No, miss,' said Dougal, 'not unless you're a doctor, even then, its use would have to be authorised by a consultant or some such before it was administered.'

'So, you reckon…'

'I reckon,' said Duncan, 'if we assume that he was an addict, then there's the distinct possibility he could've nicked the stuff from the hospital or the clinic where he was being treated.'

West thought for a moment, cradled her mug in both hands, and sipped her tea.

'Okay,' she said, 'let's have a look at that first. See if he was registered anywhere for treatment, start with his GP, maybe he got a referral somewhere, then try the rehab clinics, that sort of thing. Talk to his work colleagues, too. These rich kids never dabble alone.'

'Roger that, miss.'

'So, what do we know about him?'

'Just about everything!' said Dougal. 'He may as well have had his CV tucked into his jacket pocket. Alan Byrne. Thirty-eight years old. Single. Born Abingdon, Oxfordshire.'

'Hold on,' said West. 'Abingdon? So, he's English?'

'Aye. Apparently he spent a couple of years in Paris before being transferred over here. He works for a French investment bank on Bothwell Street, and he's got a fancy loft apartment in the Merchant City area.'

'Merchant what?' said West. 'I've never heard of it.'

'Merchant City,' said Duncan. 'It's in Glasgow. Nice place, if you've a few quid in your pocket.'

'Glasgow? Then what the hell was he doing down here?'

Duncan shrugged his shoulders and smiled.

'Not as clean-cut as you think, after all, is it?' said West. 'Anything else?'

'His car,' said Dougal. 'It's a black Range Rover, six months old with personalised plates. They found it by Sandhill Burn just off the B742, that's the road that runs by Martnaham loch. The driver's side door was open, and the keys were in the ignition.'

Taking a leaf from Munro's book in the misguided belief it may enhance her cognitive ability, West walked to the window and ran the string of beads through her fingers as she stared down at the car park.

'Not much of a view, is it?' she said, muttering to herself. 'Okay, so his car's abandoned and the keys are in the ignition. If he was off his head then he could've left the car, you know, dazed and confused, hallucinating even, and stumbled into the loch.'

'Aye, my thoughts exactly,' said Duncan confidently, 'after all, it would've been pitch-black up there and that loch would've been cold enough to freeze the…'

'Just one thing,' said Dougal, interrupting. 'If he was off his head, miss, I doubt he'd have been able to negotiate the road up to the loch in the first place.'

West turned and sighed, her nose twitching at a familiar scent.

'I recognise that smell,' she said, sniffing the beads.

'Sandalwood, miss. It keeps its fragrance for years.'

'Pity,' said Duncan, 'I can smell them from here and they're honking.'

West grinned and tossed him the beads.

'Count them,' she said.

'Are you joking me?'

'Go on.'

Unsure whether the task was relevant to the inquiry or if he was unwittingly becoming embroiled in some kind of Munro-esque parlour game, Duncan reluctantly bowed his head and began counting.

'Ninety-six, ninety-eight, one hundred, one hundred and two…'

'One hundred and eight,' said West.

'Aye! How did you…?'

'They're Mala beads. Everyone on the Holy Isle was wearing them.'

'The Holy Isle?' said Dougal. 'Were you taking religious orders or something?'

'Do me a favour. I was on a retreat trying to sort myself out. Worst week of my entire life, and that's saying something.'

'So, what's their significance?'

'Dunno, really. Something to do with Buddhists and the number of times you repeat a chant or an affirmation, I think.'

'So, you reckon this Alan Byrne was a Buddhist, maybe?'

'I doubt it. Not unless he's got a wardrobe full of orange robes to prove me wrong. Nah, it's just trendy, isn't it? A string of beads wrapped around your wrist. It won't get us anywhere. So, what about his motor? Did the SOCOs find anything juicy?'

'Not really, miss,' said Dougal as he rifled through a collection of photos. 'It was in a bit of a state: mud, slurry, grass and the like; but that's par for the course up there.'

'Right enough,' said Duncan. 'And if he was off his head, he could have just veered off the road.'

'Nothing inside?'

'Nothing to rave about. A few strands of hair and some fibres, they're with forensics for testing…'

'They're not his?'

'No,' said Dougal. 'Hair's the wrong colour and the fibres don't match what he was wearing.'

'Aye, but that could've been there for weeks,' said Duncan. 'Probably gave a pal a lift, you know?'

'Yeah, fair enough,' said West. 'Is that it?'

'Aye, afraid so,' said Dougal. 'Apart from the prints and they all belong to Byrne, so at the moment it looks as though he was definitely travelling alone.'

* * *

Sighing at the sound of footsteps along the corridor, West – fearing an unreasonable request from the larger-than-life DCI Elliot to justify their lack of progress at such an early stage of the investigation – drew a breath and braced herself for the inevitable confrontation.

'Good grief,' said Munro as he sidled into the room, 'it's like a holiday camp in here. Have I interrupted a game of snakes and ladders?'

'More like trivial pursuit,' said Duncan, grinning. 'Nice to see you, chief.'

'Aye, you too, laddie. Dougal. Charlie.'

West leaned against the window and, doing her best not to appear too happy, folded her arms and smiled.

'Where'd you leave your horse?' she said.

'My horse?'

'Well, you are the cavalry, aren't you?'

'If it's saving you're after, Charlie, I suggest you find yourself a priest. Are you in need of some help?'

'Nah, you know how it is,' said West. 'Another day, another body.'

'Is that all?'

'Yeah, no big deal, some bloke called Byrne found by the loch.'

'Nothing important, then. So, how are you all?'

'Happy as kittens,' said West. 'Dougal here is now a DS.'

'Is that so?' said Munro, smiling proudly. 'Well, good for you, laddie. Good for you, but hold on, if that's the case, then Charlie...'

'Yup. DI, same as you, so watch your step.'

Munro eased himself into a chair and, pausing as he rubbed his chin, eyed West with a look of curiosity.

'If you're a DI, Charlie,' he said, 'then that must mean that I'm...'

'In one,' said West. 'You should go see DCI Elliot as soon as you can, he's got some good news for you.'

'Has he indeed?'

'I don't believe it! After all this waiting, I thought you'd be happy!'

'Och, I am, lassie. Look at me. I'm ecstatic.'

Chapter 1

Unlike the city-dwelling hipsters who spent their nights wired to their phones streaming music or assessing the efficacy of a cabbage and baby food diet before tumbling from their beds after three hours of sleep desperate for a full-fat, four-shot, mocha latte with a caramel drizzle and a Red Bull chaser to get them on their feet again, the older and much wiser Rona Macallan – immune to the allure of caffeine and the frivolous banality of the internet – enjoyed a stress-free existence tending to her livestock, untroubled by the burden of social media and a relentless compulsion to share her schedule with the rest of the world.

Set in half an acre of rough pasture bounded by mature woodland, the former gamekeeper's cottage – with its rickety staircase, creaking floorboards, and nightly chorus of hooting owls, chattering foxes, and rutting stags – was deemed too disturbing by her partner who, in an effort to avoid recurring bouts of insomnia, spent five nights out of seven in a rented studio flat within walking distance of his office in Glasgow's city centre. This left Rona to tend to the morning chores unhindered: topping-up the water supply for the Saanen goats, ensuring the chickens – a mix of Warrens and Bantams – had plenty of feed, and refilling the hay nets for the two Highland ponies, Partick and Thistle.

Glancing up from beneath her hood, she watched as PC Billy Hayes, a prissy, middle-class urbanite with an irrational fear of anything that walked on four legs, trudged begrudgingly up the track towards her and cursed audibly as his right foot landed squarely in a pile of fresh goat droppings.

'Miss Macallan?' he said as the rain peppered his face. 'Miss Rona Macallan?'

'Aye, that's me. You took your time.'

'I came as soon as soon as I could. Have you been waiting long?'

'Since six.'

'Six o'clock? This morning?'

'When you were still in bed, no doubt.'

'Sorry, I never knew,' said Hayes. 'I only came on duty a half an hour ago, someone should've been out to see you by now. Something about vandalism, was it?'

'It's not vandalism, Constable. It's Esme.'

'Esme?'

'She's dead.'

* * *

Heeding Rona's advice, Hayes – keeping his distance – stared blankly at the kid lying on the ground and couldn't help but notice the look of utter bewilderment in its big, amber eyes and the black bolt lodged deep in the side of its neck.

'Eleven months old,' said Rona. 'Eleven months.'

Hayes, unsure of what to say or how to react, cast her a sideways glance and sighed.

'Do you mind if I take a closer look?' he said. 'If I could just…'

'I'd stay put if I were you,' said Rona, 'get too close and the other goats'll butt your backside from here to eternity.'

'Oh, they're just animals, I'm sure they'll not mind if I…'

'They're grieving!' snapped Rona. 'Just as you would be if you'd lost your sister, so I'm warning you, they'll not like it if you go sticking your nose in.'

'Well,' said Hayes, 'truth be known, that's fine by me. So, have you any idea who'd want to kill one of your goats?'

'None.'

'No arguments or quarrels with the neighbours, nobody bearing a wee grudge?'

'No.'

'Well, if that's the case, then I'm afraid to say it's probably just the local kids. Maybe one of them got a crossbow as a gift and…'

'Don't be so ridiculous,' said Rona. 'Why would a wean come all the way out here to fire one, single bolt?'

'I'm not sure, perhaps… I mean, did you not hear anything?'

'Oh aye, of course I did. The sound of a crossbow, it's enough to wake the dead.'

'Right. Point taken,' said Hayes. 'Well, to be honest, Miss Macallan, I'm really not sure what I can do about this.'

'What do you mean?'

'Well, animals, pets, livestock and such, in the eyes of the law, they're classed as chattels, possessions. They're not afforded the same rights as you and me.'

'Rubbish. I'll not have it,' said Rona. 'Just you listen to me, it's murder, pure and simple. Do you understand?'

'Aye, of course, but…'

'Look at it another way, Constable. If someone's used my Esme for target practice, then who's next on the list? Someone at the school, perhaps?'

Hayes sniffed and wiped his nose with the back of his hand as the drizzle grew heavier.

'Okay,' he said. 'If you put it like that, then I suppose whoever's responsible might be considered a risk to the public.'

'At last,' said Rona, 'I appear to be getting through. So, what happens now?'

'I'll tell you what I'll do. I'll call it in and see if I can persuade them to send another officer over, someone with more experience than me when it comes to dealing with… well, you know. Will that do you?'

'That'll do me fine, Constable,' said Rona. 'I appreciate it. But tell them to hurry up, I can't leave young Esme out here much longer. It wouldn't be right. Not right at all.'

* * *

At thirty-two years old, Craig Ferguson – a JavaScript programmer who worked for a flourishing software company in the fashionable Finnieston area of the city and earned enough to put a smile on the face of HMRC – was, with his trendy trainers, Superdry windcheater, and heavy-framed specs, somebody who embraced style over practicality and to whom a semi-rural existence was a test of endurance rather than a pleasurable way of life.

Despite his insatiable appetite and an unquenchable thirst for Tennent's lager, he managed to maintain – pot belly aside – a physique which he proudly described as slim whilst Rona, in her own inimitable way, referred to him endearingly as the runt of the litter.

Had it not been for an invitation to attend a concert by Justin Currie at Glasgow's O2 Academy three months earlier – an event blighted by the fact that she'd been hoodwinked into attending an ear-splitting gig by Franz Ferdinand rather than the sharp-suited crooner she'd fancied since her days at university – they would not have met.

Craig, similarly disgruntled as he'd forked out thirty-seven pounds on a ticket for a friend who'd failed to show up, was immediately taken by her alluring brown eyes, her wavy, copper curls and the years of back-breaking toil etched into her face.

After much persuasion – and several glasses of white wine – Rona succumbed to a date with the besotted lothario nine years her junior but only on the proviso that he travelled down to Ayr where – over a supper of smoked ham hock and mashed potatoes at the cosy 22 Bar and Grill – she was pleasantly surprised to discover that, apart from her love of yoga and the smell of horse manure, they had much in common, not least a mutual appreciation of a good book in front of a roaring fire rather than an intoxicating night in the pub.

Parking the pepper-white Mini behind Rona's 4x4 and bemoaning the fact that the pot-holed track up to the house was covered in mud rather than tarmac, thereby necessitating yet another trip to the carwash, Craig was content nonetheless to have made it back before nightfall thereby avoiding the haunting cries of the beasties in the woods that played havoc with his nyctophobic mind.

'Something smells good!' he said as he hastened inside, bolting the door behind him. 'It's not a pie, is it?'

'Casserole,' said Rona, smiling as she pecked him on the cheek. 'Venison and ale.'

'Smashing! And are we having a pudding?'

'Twin Peaks.'

'That's not meringue, is it?'

'Box set.'

'You're showing your age,' said Craig. 'I've brought the wine, four bottles. Will I open one now?'

'Aye, go on. And once you've done that, you can fetch some logs from the store outside, they're those wooden things that look like trees but without the branches.'

'In these trainers?' said Craig. 'Think again, they're brand new.'

'Never mind. So, what's the story? Busy week?'

'And then some. I've spent the last four days writing an async code in Node.js for RBS and it's been doing my head in.'

'Is that so?' said Rona, raising her glass. 'Well, you can tell me what that means, one day. At my wake, perhaps. Is that it, then? No gossip from the pub?'

'You know me, sweetheart, always in need of a bevvy after work but as for gossip, no, no. I leave that to the youngsters.'

'Hark at you!' said Rona. 'Youngsters, indeed! Best sit yourself down, granddad, you'll be in need of a rest.'

'Very funny,' said Craig. 'So, how about you? Up to your knees in horse plop again, I imagine?'

'Aye. And I've a broody bantam, a pony with colic, and the float valve on the water trough's playing-up. Oh, and Esme's dead.'

Craig, his brow furrowed with faux concern, shook his head remorsefully as though the name meant something to him.

'Too bad,' he said, glugging his wine. 'Were you close? I mean, an old school pal or something, was she?'

'She,' said Rona, rolling her eyes, 'was one of my goats.'

Trying his best not to laugh, Craig turned his back on her and snorted into his glass.

'Is that all?' he said. 'I mean, it's hardly the end of the world, is it? It's just a goat.'

Rona pulled the pot from the oven, set it on the hob, and glowered at Craig as she topped up her glass.

'Esme was eleven months old,' she said angrily. 'She walked and talked, just like you. She had a heart and a brain, just like you. And she was murdered. Shot dead. With a crossbow.'

'A crossbow? Are you sure?'

'She's in the barn. The bolt's still in her neck. You can go take a look, if you like.'

'No. You're alright,' said Craig. 'I'll take your word for it. Kids, eh? It used to be air rifles and starlings, now…'

'This wasn't some juvenile prank!' said Rona. 'This was deliberate. Of that, I'm sure.'

'Sorry,' said Craig as he reached tentatively for the bottle, 'I didn't mean to sound so, you know, callous. So, why would somebody want to kill your goat?'

Rona shrugged her shoulders.

'When did it happen?'

'This morning.'

'Did you not see who did it?'

'It was too early,' said Rona. 'Even for me. I'll wait and see what the police say, they're sending another officer tomorrow.'

Craig, his glass half way to his lips, paused and coughed as he cleared his throat.

'Another one, you say? You mean the police have been already?'

'Aye,' said Rona as she popped the plates into the oven to warm. 'This morning; only the fella that came didn't have a clue what to do, so they're sending someone else.'

'What did you tell them? I mean, did you mention me, by any chance? Not that it's important but…'

'No. As it happens, I'm afraid your name did not pop up in the conversation.'

'Good.'

'Why?'

'Oh, no reason. Just wondering.'

'What's going on here, Craig?' said Rona, her hackles rising. 'This is not about the money is it? I thought you said that was sorted.'

'It's not about the money!' said Craig tersely as he zipped his coat and turned for the door, 'There's something I have to do, that's all. I'll be as quick as I can. Now lock the door and don't wait up.'

Chapter 2

Both respected and revered for the reputation he'd garnered as a ruthless, young DS who – rulebook aside – had fearlessly faced-up to even the most hardened of criminals, the effervescent DCI George Elliot, known affectionately as "the bear" amongst the lower ranks was, despite his notoriety, the kind of laidback boss any serving officer would have given their eye teeth to work under.

Bored with the mundane task of assessing a pile of performance reviews, he brushed them aside and grinned as Munro peered sheepishly round the door.

'James!' he said. 'This is a surprise!'

'You're looking well, George,' said Munro as he pulled up a chair. 'Paperwork obviously suits you.'

'It does indeed, James! I'm glad you're here, I've been meaning to talk to you.'

'Have you indeed?'

'Aye, I wish you'd said you were coming, though, we could've had lunch – Cechinni's!'

'Och, I wasnae planning on coming in, George, I've just dropped by to collect...'

'The good news?'

'…my belongings, but as you've mentioned it, what's this good news, then?'

'Brace yourself, James,' said Elliot excitedly. 'Brace yourself! As we say in our line of work; you're free to go!'

Munro, regarding Elliot with a feigned look of confusion, leaned back and folded his arms.

'Free to go, as in, relieved of your duties! You're officially retired! Good God, man, I thought you'd be pleased.'

'Delirious.'

Elliot, taking Munro's deadpan delivery as par for the course, hauled his heavy frame from the chair and retrieved a bottle of Cordon Rouge from the fridge.

'I bought you this,' he said, plonking it on the table. 'I thought we'd raise a glass to your future. Will we go next door and crack it open?'

'That's very generous of you, George,' said Munro, raising his hand, 'but not just now, I've the car outside and…'

'As you wish, James. As you wish. You can take it with you. What say we catch up next week? Wednesday, perhaps? Or Thursday? Friday, even. Fridays are good.'

'We'll see,' said Munro. 'Let me get the house sorted out first, everything's in a wee bit of a muddle. You understand.'

'Of course I do. You let me know when's convenient and we'll all go out. You, me, Charlie, Dougal, and Duncan. That's assuming no dead bodies turn up, of course.'

'Aye. Of course. I'll give you a call.'

'I'll look forward to it. Now, I hope you don't think I'm being rude, but I really must dash. Mrs Elliot's expecting me home at any moment. She's been experimenting with something called a NutriBullet. Have you any idea what a NutriBullet is?'

'It sounds like a healthy version of Russian roulette,' said Munro. 'You'd best get going, as I recall your wife's not one for tardiness.'

'You're not wrong there, James,' said Elliot as he handed Munro a slip of paper. 'A wee favour, if I may. Would you give this to one of the lads, it's an address for a lady over in Cumnock. I'm told she's had a wee bit of bother on her farm. Ask them to look into it, would you? And I'll see you next week.'

* * *

Munro, looking as cheerful as a cheesemaker with a lactose intolerance, ambled back to the office and sighed as he placed the bottle on the desk.

'Bloody hell,' said West, 'you look like you've just been sacked, not given a golden handshake.'

'Dour, lassie,' said Munro, 'it's my natural expression. As I've told you before, I'm not happy unless I'm being miserable.'

'You must be ecstatic then. At least you've got some champagne.'

'Aye, but it's not for me, really. You lot can have it.'

'I'll pass if you don't mind, boss,' said Dougal. 'No offence, but alcohol and me don't get along.'

'I'm not that keen on the fizz, either,' said West. 'A decent red or a drop of your Balvenie's more my cup of tea.'

'Well, that leaves you then, laddie,' said Munro as he sat down and loosened his tie. 'Or do you have an aversion to bubbles, as well?'

'No, no, I can handle the bubbles, chief,' said Duncan, 'but I'm not taking that off you. That was a gift.'

'Tell me, Duncan, have you any plans for the weekend?'

'The weekend? Well, aye, I'm away to Girvan to see Cathy, she's arranged a babysitter so we can…'

'Then, as far as I'm concerned,' said Munro, 'that's a good enough reason to celebrate. You have it, take it with my compliments. Now, it's time I was off.'

'Hold on,' said West. 'Aren't you forgetting something?'

Munro thought for a moment, frowned, and slowly shook his head.

'No, Charlie,' he said. 'I cannae think of anything.'

'Dinner?'

'Dinner?'

'Yes! You agreed,' said West, lying through her teeth. 'Come on. I'm all out of food so it'll have to be the chippy. We can grab some wine on the way.'

'Wine? Och, I cannae drink, Charlie. I'm driving.'

'Then you'll have to stay over, won't you? No arguments, let's go.'

* * *

It didn't take Munro's sixth sense to realise that their pre-arranged dinner date was nothing more than an impulsive act of compassion designed to alleviate their mutual boredom but Munro was, nonetheless, grateful for the invitation which also provided him with the perfect excuse for avoiding the builders who, though industrious to a fault, clearly preferred working on his house rather than returning to their own, even after dark.

Back in the familiar surroundings of her apartment on North Harbour Street, he stood on the balcony, hands tucked behind his back, and gazed trance-like at the setting sun while West, as hungry as a love-starved puppy, unpacked two fish suppers, a bottle of red, and a giant Toblerone.

'Oi, Jimbo!' she said. 'Don't just stand there, brown sauce and a couple of glasses, please – quick as you can.'

Munro willingly obliged, poured the wine, and joined West at the table as she crammed a forkful of chips into her mouth.

'Well,' she said, raising her glass, 'that's that then. Cheers.'

'That's what then?' said Munro, his face a picture of gloom.

'You. Finito. Out to grass.'

'You have a way with words, Charlie, you know that? Have you not thought about a career with the Samaritans?'

'You know what I mean,' said West with a smirk. 'Seriously though, have you thought about what you're going to do once the house is finished?'

'I cannae plan that far ahead, lassie,' said Munro, 'they've not even got the roof on yet. Then there's the windows to fit, then the plastering and the tiling, and then the new kitchen. All that before I can even give it a lick of paint.'

'Must be a pain in the backside.'

'Aye. Like a bad case of piles. The worst part though, apart from the infernal racket, is that they're still at it when normal folk should be in their beds.'

'Really? I thought all builders knocked off at three o'clock.'

'Not these lads,' said Munro. 'Edison gave them the gift of light and they're intent on using it.'

'Best thing you can do,' said West as she helped herself to another glass, 'is move out for a bit. Let them get on with it.'

'My thoughts exactly, Charlie. That's why I'm thinking of taking that cottage on Skye for a month or two.'

'I've got a better idea,' said West. 'You can crash here.'

Munro polished off the last of his haddock, took a large sip of wine and stared blankly at West.

'No, no,' he said. 'Don't get me wrong, Charlie, it's not that I'm not grateful for the offer, but I'll not impose. Not again.'

'Too late,' said West. 'I've already made up the spare bed, there's a toothbrush and a razor in the bathroom, and

I've washed the clothes that you left behind. All you have to do is nip back home and fetch some more.'

'You had this all planned, didn't you?'

'Me? Don't be silly.'

'Then what's with the washing?' said Munro. 'I know you, Charlie, domesticity is not in your genes.'

'No, but looking after mates is. Anyway, I'm being selfish really. I thought you might like to help out. Unofficially, that is.'

'Help out? Sorry, Charlie, but I'm not a housemaid.'

'I don't mean cleaning,' said West. 'I mean work, proper work. Best you keep that brain of yours ticking over, I don't want you going all senile on me.'

* * *

Munro, suitably refreshed after a sound night's sleep, rose as usual at five-thirty and, wary of waking his host, made his way silently to the kitchen with the intention of brewing a pot of tea when the sight of a bleary-eyed West seated at the table crunching her way through a mountain of buttered toast stopped him dead in his tracks.

'Jumping Jehoshaphat!' he said. 'I must be dreaming.'

'Toast?'

'I've got to hand it to you, Charlie, I never thought I'd see the day when you'd be up at this hour, unless of course you've not been to bed?'

'I picked up a few tips from a crotchety, old cop…'

'Careful.'

'…and he was right. The earlier you get up, the more you get done.'

'I think I'm going to have a seizure.'

'Relax, I'm kidding.'

'Thank God for that.'

'I got a call,' said West, 'well a text actually, from Dougal.'

'Is that about the Byrne fellow? By the loch?'

'Nope. It's something completely different. They found a car on the A76 southbound last night. A few miles north of Mauchline. Do you know it?'

'Aye, it's not far.'

'One occupant, the driver. He's now in the ICU and by all accounts, barely breathing.'

'Sorry, Charlie, you're losing me. Is this not something uniform should be dealing with?'

'Afraid not, Jimbo. According to Dougal, this wasn't an RTC. They reckon the bloke must've passed out while he was driving and crashed off the road.'

'Passed out? What was it? Asthma? A heart attack?'

'Not quite,' said West. 'You've heard of *Fifty Shades of Grey*, well this bloke was fifty shades of black and blue. Had the crap knocked out of him, by the sounds of it.'

'Dear, dear, dear. So the poor chap was assaulted before trying to make his way home?'

'Seems that way,' said West as she slipped her phone into her hip holster and pulled on her jacket. 'We'll soon find out. You ready? We have to pick up Dougal first.'

'Ready?' said Munro, smiling as he snatched a slice of toast from her plate. 'No, no, no, Charlie, you forget, I am now a man of leisure. You can fill me in when you get back, after which this crotchety, old cop may impart some words of wisdom, should you need them, of course.'

'I take it that means you're not coming, then?'

'I am not.'

'Well, I hope you're not going to sit around here moping all day.'

'I'll do no such thing,' said Munro. 'As soon as I've had a brew, I shall drive to the supermarket and fetch some provisions, your fridge is woefully empty. Then I shall nip home and pack a bag.'

'Good, you'll need these, then,' said West as she tossed him a spare set of keys. 'I'll catch you, later.'

'Oh, Charlie, before you go, you'd best have this.'

Munro reached into his trouser pocket and pulled out a small, silver flip-phone no larger than a credit card.

'I don't believe it,' said West, 'you've finally got yourself a phone.'

'How else would I keep track of the builders?'

'Where'd you get it? The Science Museum?'

'It makes calls and it sends texts, lassie. That's all I need. Now, I'll give you a call and hang up, then you'll have my number. I've a funny feeling you'll be needing it.'

Chapter 3

Much to Dougal's disappointment the boat trip to Ailsa Craig had proved to be a much bigger draw for local families than the unattached, back-packing, wildlife enthusiasts he'd expected, whilst the annual dinner-dance at the fishing club which boasted several young ladies amongst its members had been marred by the overwhelming presence of married couples. But the ceilidh for singles only – where the men outnumbered the women by three to one – was perhaps the most depressing event he'd ever attended in his quest to find a partner who shared his love of books and his dislike of alcohol.

Tragically optimistic that his soulmate might be working in the A&E department of the local hospital, Dougal – dressed in his neatly pressed jeans, sensible leather shoes and beige blouson – was waiting outside the police station when West, seemingly oblivious to the function of the brake pedal, mounted the kerb in her Figaro forcing him to jump for cover.

'Alright, Dougal!' she yelled. 'Hop in!'

Having learned from experience that West was exceptionally proficient at handling her car like a rallycross driver, Dougal took a deep breath and slipped nervously into the passenger seat.

'Morning, miss,' he said as he buckled-up. 'How are you?'

'Tired. I don't know how you do it, Dougal, getting up this early. It's not natural.'

'Don't blame me, blame mother nature. I think it has something to do with the body clock.'

'If that's true, then mine's stuck on snooze. You okay?'

'Aye, all good,' said Dougal. 'You can slow down, if you like. We've plenty of time yet.'

'Yeah, you're right,' said West. 'No point in rushing, is there? After all, it sounds like this bloke, whoever he is, isn't going to be getting out of bed for a while yet.'

Dougal, relieved to see the speedometer dip below forty miles an hour, settled back and tried his best to relax.

'How's the boss?' he said. 'Is he doing alright?'

'Jimbo? Yeah, I think so.'

'It'll not be the same without him, now that he's retired, I mean.'

'Oh, you haven't seen the last of him, I can guarantee it.'

'I hope you're right. I worry about him, he's not one for being idle. If he's time on his hands, he'll start climbing the wall.'

'I've thought about that,' said West, stifling a yawn. 'I think we'll throw him a few scraps to keep him busy. What do you think?'

'I think that's a brilliant idea.'

'Good. So, no plans for the weekend?'

'No plans, full stop.'

'Just as well this turned up, eh? Something to keep us all out of trouble.'

* * *

'He's the tall, skinny fella in triage,' said the girl on the desk. 'You can't miss him, he's the one that looks like death. White shirt. Short sleeves, and a look of despair.'

At forty-six years old, Doctor Mark Bowen – a dedicated junior registrar nearing the end of yet another twelve-hour shift – stood by the bed and, doing his utmost not to unleash a torrent of abuse, politely advised the inebriated woman with a broken stiletto that it was nothing more than a mild sprain and how she'd be better off resting her ankle in the comfort of her own home rather than occupying one of his much-needed beds.

He glanced round and glowered at West as she lingered outside the bay, his eyes a startling shade of Scandinavian grey.

'Can I help?' he said, expecting a complaint.

'Hope so,' said West. 'The girl on the desk said we'd find you here. Are you in charge?'

'Aye. Mark Bowen. Registrar.'

'Don't mean to sound rude but you look as bad as I feel.'

'Trust me,' said Bowen, 'no-one can feel that bad. How can I help?'

'Sorry. DI West. And this is DS McCrae. It's about a bloke who was brought in last night.'

Bowen despatched the woman to the waiting area to have her ankle bandaged by a nurse and closed the curtain as West perched on the edge of the bed and smiled.

'Busy night?' she said.

'Just the usual,' said Bowen, tousling his mop of unruly hair. 'Same old story, folk who can't handle their drink but at least nobody pissed on the floor or threatened my staff. I've that to look forward to.'

'Is it always that bad?' said Dougal.

'Aye, Sergeant, it is. Especially Saturday nights. That's when it all kicks off.'

'I don't envy you. At least we can just lock them up.'

'You've no idea how lucky you are. So, who are you after?'

'Haven't got a name,' said West. 'His car went off the road just outside Mauchline, last night. All we know is, he was beaten to a pulp.'

'Oh, him,' said Bowen, despondently. 'He's in the ICU and he's not looking good, I'm afraid.'

'Go on.'

'Let me think. As I recall, he has a broken jaw, two fractured cheek bones, a fractured eye socket, broken collar bone, not to mention a few ribs, severe bruising to the abdomen, oh, and a trauma to the back of the head. There's a good chance he has a bleed on the brain but we can't move him to check, not just now.'

'Blimey,' said West. 'So, he didn't just walk into a lamp post then, did he?'

'A couple of baseball bats, more like.'

'Have you any idea if he'd been drinking?' said Dougal. 'Or if he was on anything?'

'The only thing he's on is life support but, as we had to fit a catheter, I took the liberty of sending a sample for testing but I doubt if we'll get it back before Monday.'

'Was he conscious when he came in?' said West. 'Did he say anything?'

'Not a peep, the man was out cold.'

'So, we've no chance of having a word?'

'Not unless you're telepathic,' said Bowen. 'Even then I wouldn't hold out much hope. In fact, I hate to be the bearer of bad news, but I can't say for certain if he'll even pull through. You should speak to the consultant about his prognosis.'

'Pants,' said West. 'Not a good start for us, is it? Oh, hold on, was he carrying any ID? I mean, you must have stripped him before…'

'Oh, aye. A wallet and a few bits and bobs, I think.'

'And I suppose uniform took them, did they?'

27

'No, no. I sent them packing, they were getting in the way. All his stuff's bagged up. Will I get a nurse to fetch it for you?'

'Yes, please,' said West as she pulled a card from her pocket and handed it over. 'Give us a call if anything happens, would you? We'll drop by tomorrow to check on his progress, oh, and get yourself something to eat, you look like you could do with it.'

'Is that an invitation?' said Bowen, raising his eyebrows.

'Maybe,' said West as she walked away. 'Maybe.'

* * *

Dougal, looking unusually sombre, fastened his safety belt, folded his arms and sighed as though he were carrying the weight of the world on his shoulders.

'You okay?' said West. 'Are you upset about the bloke who…?'

'No, no. It's not that, miss, it's…'

'Go on. If something's up, you can tell me.'

'No, you're alright. You'll only laugh.'

'Won't. Promise.'

'Well,' said Dougal, 'how come… how come it's so easy for you? I mean, like just then, getting asked out on a date?'

'What?' said West, laughing. 'He did no such thing.'

'Aye, of course he did. Just not in so many words.'

'Don't talk rubbish.'

'I'm serious. That doctor could hardly take his eyes off you.'

'Well, it must be down to my ravishing good looks, then,' said West, grinning. 'And the fact that I'm sexy as hell.'

'Sorry I asked. So, what now? We'll not be getting any joy out of the fella in ICU anytime soon.'

'Mauchline,' said West. 'We should take a look at the car.'

* * *

As someone who regarded shopping as a necessary evil made all the more tedious by folk who insisted on dawdling along the aisles browsing items they neither liked nor needed, Munro – not usually one for sniffing out bargains – was nonetheless feeling suitably smug at discovering the supermarket's offer of "three for ten pounds" on a quite respectable Côtes du Rhône.

He parked the trolley by the car, popped open the boot and placed all twelve bottles inside, along with two large carriers packed to the hilt with bacon and eggs, potatoes, oven chips, several sirloin steaks, a token packet of chicken breasts, two roasting joints, an assortment of snacks, and a bottle of Balvenie before fumbling for his glasses and pulling out the slip of paper DCI Elliot had handed him the day before.

'By jiminy,' he said, muttering under his breath. 'Perhaps I am losing it after all.'

* * *

Following the closure of the railway line, which – along with the demise of the ironworks, the coal mines, the tweed factories, and the pottery – should have sounded the death knell for the once thriving market town, Cumnock had instead evolved into a burgeoning borough with more than its fair share of restaurants, coffee shops, gyms and nail bars, and even a factory outlet flogging designer goods at knock-down prices, all of which Munro – who was as keen on progress as the Huli Wigmen of Papua New Guinea – avoided by negotiating the bypass to the comparative tranquillity of the surrounding countryside.

Smiling as he spied a weathered sign proclaiming "Tèarmann" hanging from a five-bar gate, he weaved his way through the clumps of silage, eased the Peugeot up the muddy drive and waved politely as Rona – curious about the unexpected visitor – slowly made her way towards him.

'Sanctuary,' he said as he stepped from the car and zipped his coat. 'It has a nice ring to it.'

'You know your Gaelic, then?'

'Well, it wouldnae be my specialist subject on Mastermind,' said Munro with a smile, 'but I do remember some from school.'

'It's the name given to the lodge when this was all a part of the Lochnorris estate, centuries ago.'

'Is that so? Miss Macallan, is it?'

'It is, aye. And you are?'

'Munro. James Munro.'

'Of course,' said Rona. 'I should've guessed. Police, right?'

'Well, no, not exactly, you see…'

'I've been expecting you. Come with me. She's in the barn.'

'She?'

'Esme. She's dead.'

'Dead?'

'Aye, did they not tell you?'

'No,' said a bewildered Munro. 'No, they did not.'

'Never mind. Eleven months old, she was. Can you believe it? Eleven months.'

'Good grief! What was it? A cot death?'

Rona turned to Munro and laughed out loud.

'No, it's not a cot death, Mr Munro…'

'Thank goodness for that.'

'…she was murdered.'

Munro, the colour draining from his cheeks, froze on the spot, his brow furrowed with confusion.

'Murdered?' he said. 'Miss Macallan, I fear we may be at cross-purposes here, would you mind…?'

'Esme. She's one of my goats.'

* * *

Munro, far from relieved that the body in question was not that of a child, solemnly shook his head as Rona pulled back the tarpaulin to reveal the lifeless carcass.

'Dear, dear, dear,' he said, shocked at the sight of the bolt protruding from the side of her neck. 'Who in God's name would do such a thing? To a defenceless animal?'

'I've no idea,' said Rona, 'but whoever it was needs locking up.'

'You're not wrong there,' said Munro with a hefty sigh. 'I'll be frank with you, Miss Macallan, this is exactly the kind of thing that turns my stomach – more than finding some scally with a bullet hole in the back of his head.'

'Then we're two of kind,' said Rona. 'People I can live without.'

'You and me both. So, this happened yesterday, is that correct?'

'Aye, early hours, before I was up.'

'So, that would have been when?'

'Any time before five.'

'And that's when you found her?'

'Thereabouts,' said Rona, 'I came out around a half-past. The rest of the herd were kicking up a stink...'

'I'm not surprised.'

'...so at first I thought she was just ill, then I saw the bolt and called the police straight away.'

'So, you know the bolt's from a crossbow, then?'

'Oh, aye. Well, it's not going to be a bow and arrow, is it?'

'No, no,' said Munro, smiling, 'you're quite right, of course. Pardon the question but I have to ask, do you happen to own one?'

'A crossbow? I most certainly do not.'

'Good. Well, I can tell you this, Miss Macallan,' said Munro as he leaned in for a closer look, 'this bolt's one of the wee ones, about six inches in length, so it would've been fired from a pistol bow.'

'A pistol bow?' said Rona. 'What's that?'

'The clue's in the title. It's not a big thing the likes of William Tell would've used to shoot apples off a wean's head. These are small enough to be fired with one hand.'

'I see. Then I don't understand,' said Rona. 'If they fired it like a gun, then they must've come up the drive, and if they did that, then why did they not spook the herd?'

'Believe it not,' said Munro, 'those wee pistols have quite a range on them; forty, fifty, maybe even sixty feet.'

Munro stood by the doors of the barn and pointed across the meadow towards the house.

'See here, Miss Macallan,' he said, 'there's no line of sight from here to the drive but you can see the road. I imagine that's where it was fired from.'

'But why?'

'That's what we'll try to find out,' said Munro as he turned to Esme and pulled out his phone. 'I need to take a couple of... blast! I forgot, my phone doesnae have a camera.'

'Will I do it?' said Rona. 'Then I can send you the photos.'

'Aye, that's good of you, thanks. I shall need some close-up, different angles, and a couple including her head and neck. Tell me, Miss Macallan, have you had any bother with the neighbours around here? Or anyone in town, perhaps?'

'No, none. And that's what I told the cop who was here yesterday.'

'And did he proffer any suggestions as to who the perpetrator might be?'

'Kids, would you believe?'

Munro smiled reassuringly at Rona.

'No. It's not kids,' he said, 'but you knew that, already. Kids wouldnae come all the way out here in the dead of night just to shoot one goat and run away. I'm sorry to say it, but this was deliberate.'

'Which brings me back to my original question, Mr Munro: why?'

'To which I replied: I'll try to find out.'

Rona smiled, pulled her coat across her chest and began the walk back to the house.

'Can I offer you some tea before you go?' she said. 'Or a coffee, maybe?'

'No, no, you're alright,' said Munro, 'but thanks all the same. Tell me, Miss Macallan, what is it you farm here, exactly?'

'Och, it's not a farm. More of a smallholding, really. I only have the goats and the chickens. They keep a roof over my head.'

'And how's that?'

'Cheese, butter, and milk. And eggs from the chickens, of course. It's all organic, mind. I sell locally.'

'A proper cottage industry, just like the old days. Most commendable. Most commendable, indeed.'

'I'll fetch you some if you like, you're welcome to try it. The goats' cheese is especially tasty.'

'I'll take your word for it,' said Munro. 'I'm more of a cheddar man, myself.'

'Well, the offer's there, if you change your mind.'

'Will I stay and lend you a hand? I mean, would you like some help laying Esme to rest?'

'No, it's fine, really,' said Rona. 'I've already dug her a nice spot out near the woods. It's sunny there, she'll like it. So, what happens now?'

Munro hesitated as he opened the car door.

'The bolt,' he said decisively. 'We'll start with the bolt. It should be relatively easy to trace, particularly if it was bought locally, after all, a pistol bow's not exactly common, is it?'

'Right you are. So, when will I hear from you?'

'Och, I wouldnae hold your breath, Miss Macallan, these things take time. I'll be in touch when I have something to report. Oh, and here's a card, you can send the photos to the address on that.'

Chapter 4

Rummaging through the cupboards in a desperate search for something to eat other than the bananas she'd bought purely as a table decoration, West – embarrassed at not being able to offer Dougal even a Hobnob – yelped with delight as the front door opened and a weary-looking Munro, doing a passable impression of a packhorse on the Pampas, lumbered down the hallway with his holdall slung across his shoulders and his arms straining with the weight of the shopping bags and the wine carriers.

'At last!' she said as she launched herself at the groceries like a rapacious wolf, 'we're absolutely starving.'

'No change there, then.'

'Where the hell have you been?'

'Guess,' said Munro as he pulled the Balvenie from one of the bags. 'And you're most welcome. Not a bother.'

'Sorry, I mean, thanks. You shouldn't have. Hasn't taken you this long, though, surely?'

'No, no. As you can see, I went to fetch some clothes as well. Dougal, nice to see you, laddie. Are you well?'

'Aye, thanks boss,' said Dougal peering over the laptop. 'All good.'

'And what, if I might ask, are you so engrossed in?'

'I invited him for dinner,' said West, 'so he could help me out. We're trying to trace a phone number.'

'Are you indeed?' said Munro as he poured himself a whisky. 'And is this something to do with the fellow in the hospital?'

'Worse. I think I've been sent death threats by some Pagan cult.'

'What?'

'Here,' said West as she passed him her phone. 'Some weirdo's sent me a stack of photos of a dead goat.'

Munro, not usually given to overt displays of jocularity, burst into fits of laughter.

'What's so funny?' said West, snatching the phone. 'This is serious! It's sick!'

'Did you not get any of a virgin lying on the sacrificial altar?'

'You know something, don't you?'

'I'll explain, lassie. I'll explain. You see, yesterday, when I saw George, he asked me to pass on an address, to yourself in fact, Dougal, but I forgot.'

'An address for what, boss?'

'A woman over in Cumnock,' said Munro, gasping as the Balvenie hit the back of his throat, 'she's had some trouble at home. I found the address in my pocket this morning and as the pair of you were otherwise engaged, and Duncan's away with his latest squeeze, I took it upon myself to pay her a wee visit.'

'So, what's this got to do with a satanic death cult?' said West.

'It's nothing of the sort, Charlie. Some demented individual killed one of her goats, with a crossbow no less. Hence the photographs.'

'Oh, that's too bad,' said Dougal. 'He's obviously not right in the head, is he?'

'Yeah, but hold on, hold on,' said West. 'Animals are possessions, right? So, why did DCI Elliot ask you, I mean Dougal, to look into it?'

'I've no idea,' said Munro, 'but orders are orders.'

'Well, I don't get it. I mean, there's bugger all we can do about a dead goat.'

'On the contrary, lassie, there's plenty we can do. This lady, her name's Rona Macallan by the way, was clearly quite upset, not least because it affects her livelihood, too.'

'Livelihood?' said West, scouring the worktops for a corkscrew. 'Don't tell me she breeds goats?'

'She makes cheese, lassie. And butter.'

'Well, whoop-de-do. Even so...'

'Even so,' said Munro. 'I said I'd look into it for her.'

'You can't, Jimbo! You're retired!'

'And you're busy. I may not be a DI anymore, Charlie, but there's nothing to stop me being a PI.'

'Oh, come off it, you can't be serious.'

'Alright then,' said Munro as he pulled a plastic bag from his pocket containing the steel-tipped bolt, 'let's just say it's a wee favour for a friend. A fellow animal lover. Dougal, this was fired from the crossbow. Now, as you have a computer, and I do not, I wonder if you'd mind trying to find out where it came from.'

'Aye, okay boss. Let's have it here. It must have a manufacturer's marque on it somewhere.'

'Just a moment,' said West, smirking. 'That's using police resources without authority.'

'What do mean, Charlie?'

'Dougal, of course. He's one of my resources.'

'You've become quite possessive in your dotage, lassie,' said Munro, 'however, as it's the weekend, and Dougal's a grown man, I think it's only right we let him decide how he spends his downtime.'

'I don't mind, miss, really,' said Dougal. 'I've nothing else to do.'

'Well done, laddie, I knew I could count on you. Now, if you're stopping for supper, will you take a steak with us, or will I do you some chicken?'

'No, no, not for me. Change of plan, boss. I'd rather get my teeth into this.'

'Oh, come on Dougal,' said West, 'it's the least we can do. There's plenty to go round.'

'Thanks, but no. I'll take myself off and do this at home. I can work better without distractions. I'd say this has probably come from one of those sporting shops. I'll have a look for stockists in the area first, then widen the search.'

'Good luck with that,' said West, sarcastically.

'Sorry?'

'Look, if someone's going round hunting farm animals, they're hardly likely to go into a shop and say, "can I have some arrows for my crossbow, please".'

'Your point being, Charlie?'

'The internet?'

Munro drained his glass, smiled at West, and winked.

'My, my, you are sharpening up, lassie, but let's start with the shops first, it's easier and quicker. Besides, if that bolt was ordered off the internet, then I doubt we've any chance of tracing it at all.'

'I'm with you, boss,' said Dougal as he reached for his crash helmet, 'if it was off the internet, then we're humped. Are we away to the hospital tomorrow, miss?'

'Yeah, we should see how the poor bloke's doing,' said West, 'but it's pointless the both of us going. I'll do it. You concentrate on that.'

'Okay, you know where I'll be if you need me.'

West poured two generous glasses of red and set about unpacking the groceries as Munro slung his coat over a chair and sat down, relieved to take the weight off his feet.

'So,' he said, sipping his wine. 'How was your day, Charlie? Did you actually get to speak with the chap in the hospital?'

'Unfortunately not,' said West. 'The poor sod's in the ICU. The only thing keeping him alive is the national grid.'

'Dear, dear. So, you've no leads then?'

'Actually, yeah, we do. We know his name's Ferguson. Craig Ferguson. He's a thirty-something with a flash new Mini and two platinum credit cards. Glasgow are sending the boys round to his flat to see if there's anyone there. Hopefully he's got a wife, or a girlfriend, or something.'

'Glasgow?'

'Yup. That's where he lives, and works. Well, according to his driving licence it is. And he was carrying a security pass for some techy company on Finnieston Street.'

'Well, what on earth was he doing down here if he's based in Glasgow?'

'I wish I knew,' said West. 'Maybe he's got family in the area. We'll just have to wait until he wakes up, if he wakes up, to find out.'

Munro leaned back, held the glass to lips and pondered the scenario.

'They found his vehicle in Mauchline, you say?'

'Just outside,' said West, 'but he was definitely heading in this direction. And before you ask, the car was clean. We're working back along the road until we get some cameras, then, if we can pick him up, we should be able to find out exactly where he came from.'

Munro took a large sip of wine and smiled contentedly.

'Charlie, Charlie, Charlie,' he said wistfully.

'I heard you the first time.'

'Do you recall the day we met? That fateful day you wandered into my office looking for help?'

'Yeah, of course I do. I was trying to trace a missing person. Some bar owner who lived in Wanstead.'

'And do you remember what a complete and utter mess you were in?'

'Pardon?'

'Havering into your vodka every night and living off takeaways? Hiding from your responsibilities?'

'Thanks for reminding me.'

'And just look at you now.'

'What are you getting at?'

'You, lassie. You've changed. Matured. Dare I say, grown up, even. There's no doubt about it, you've come a long way, Charlie. A long way indeed.'

'Oh, stop it. If it wasn't for the fact you'd spent most of your time booting me up the backside, I'd have jacked it in ages ago.'

'And is that how you feel now? Like jacking it in?'

West leaned against the fridge folded her arms and smiled ruefully.

'Nah. To be honest, Jimbo, since moving up here I'm actually enjoying it. For the first time ever, I'm actually enjoying it. Although, I have to say, not having to work with a team of misogynistic layabouts pumped full of testosterone does help.'

'Good. Then we should celebrate. One steak or two?'

Chapter 5

For the second time in as many days, Munro – who'd witnessed some truly harrowing scenes throughout his forty-year career including dismembered bodies scattered across the railway tracks, dead junkies lying in their own filth, and a rotting corpse washed up with the tide – was not prepared for the sight of West lounging on the sofa in her Minnie Mouse pyjamas snacking on pitta and houmous with her laptop balancing on her tummy at such an early hour.

'Please tell me that's a film you're watching, Charlie, and nothing to do with work. I'm not sure my heart will stand the shock.'

'Then you'd better get yourself a pacemaker, Jimbo. It's work, I'm afraid.'

'In that case I'm in need of a strong brew and a sit down. Will I fetch you a cup?'

'No, ta. Got one here.'

'I've been thinking,' said Munro as he pulled up a chair and stirred three spoons of sugar into his tea, 'this chap, the fellow in the motor car, you said he lives and works in Glasgow?'

'Nothing wrong with your memory.'

'But he was found on the southbound carriageway just outside Mauchline?'

'That's right.'

'Okay, so, this fellow's had seven bells knocked out of him, right? Why then did he not go home? Or to the A&E? Why was he heading down here?'

'Dunno,' said West. 'Maybe he's on the run, maybe he was legging it south of the border, you know, Carlisle, or Leeds, or London.'

'No, no, not in his condition.'

'Well, maybe he was scared, just trying to get away.'

'From whom?'

'Sorry, Jimbo, too early. I'll get back to you on that one.'

'No, no,' said Munro. 'Mark my words, Charlie, this Ferguson chappie knows someone round here. Trust me. I'd start searching, if I were you.'

'I'll send the sniffer dogs out as soon as I've finished this.'

'Finished what? Have you had news from the hospital?'

'Nah, it's an email,' said West, 'from Glasgow. The good news is, they've saved me a shedload of work.'

'How so?'

'They picked up Ferguson's Mini double-parked outside a bar on Argyle Street, not far from where he works.'

'Perhaps it's his local, or an after-work watering hole.'

'Could be,' said West, 'either way, he must've said something to upset someone. The cameras outside caught him staggering from Corunna Street, that's one door down, and he's in a right state. That must be where he was done-over.'

'And the time?'

'About fifty minutes before they found him, so it ties in perfectly, he was heading down here straight from the bar, no stopping along the way.'

'Well, you seem to have everything under control,' said Munro as he finished his tea and reached for his coat. 'Don't take this the wrong way, I mean, I'm not teaching you to suck eggs but I'd call the bar if I were you, see if he was meeting anyone, find out who he talked to.'

'At this hour? On a Sunday?'

'Quite right, I'm getting ahead of myself. Well, that's me away. I'll see you this evening.'

'Hold on,' said West, 'what do you mean? Where are you going?'

'Home. I need to speak with the builders about the plans for the new kitchen before they rip out the old one. Oh, and speaking of kitchens, I thought we'd have some roast beef for supper, what do you say?'

'Smashing.'

'Good. If you put it on at five, we can eat at seven.'

* * *

Dougal, enjoying a Sunday brunch of soft boiled eggs and a round of toast and marmalade as he continued his internet search for shops that specialised in field sports or outdoor pursuits, was momentarily distracted by an arresting image of a busty brunette in khaki shorts wielding a hunting rifle in one hand and a brace of pheasants in the other who was, according to the headline, "a game bird with attitude".

Embarrassed, he promptly returned to the search page and concentrated his efforts on the text-based listings, lest he be drawn into joining a gun club in the vain hope of meeting a sharp-shooting singleton at target practice, when an unexpected call interrupted his train of thought.

'Has something happened?' he said. 'It's not like you to call on a Sunday.'

'Relax, there's nothing wrong, pal,' said Duncan. 'In fact, I'd go so far as to say things couldn't be better.'

'So, the champagne went down okay?'

'Oh, aye. More than okay, I've left her sleeping it off.'

'Alright for some. So, what's the story?'

'Just thought I'd check in,' said Duncan. 'I'm heading back home, I need to clear my head before I start trying to trace the source of the Buprenorphine they found in that Byrne fella.'

'No offence, Duncan, but what's with the enthusiasm?'

'Well, I've not got the chief to cushion my fall anymore, have I? I have to answer to Westy now, so I thought I'd best start behaving myself. How about you? Anything happening I should know about?'

'Not unless you're interested in goats,' said Dougal.

'What are you havering about?'

'One was shot with a crossbow yesterday, over in Cumnock. The DCI's asked us to look into it.'

'The DCI? Why? Is he up for making a curry or something?'

'I've no idea but the boss…'

'Munro? But he's retired now.'

'That's what we thought. Anyway, he went to see the owner and he brought back the bolt, I'm trying to find out where it came from.'

'A crossbow, you say? That's not the weapon of choice for your average nutter. It's probably someone who's into archery or paintballing, I reckon.'

'Aye, could be,' said Dougal. 'I never thought of that.'

'You should check it out. See here, when I was up in Inverkip, some of the lads used to go to a place near Paisley. They were well into it.'

'Did you take part?'

'Me?' said Duncan laughing aloud. 'No, no. Run around with a bunch of wee fellas playing at being soldiers? That's not for me. I can think of better ways of getting my kicks than chasing some numpty through the woods with a toy gun.'

'They've probably got some kind of inferiority complex,' said Dougal, 'but paintball's one thing, Duncan, this is completely different.'

'Nonsense, pal, it's all the same. Listen, I'll give them a call if you like, see if any of them are into crossbows. It'll not do any harm. I mean, they might even know where to get the ammo from.'

* * *

Dressed in black jeans, a white vest and her well-worn, waxed cotton jacket, West – her ruffled hair pinned precariously atop her head – checked her phone as she waited in reception for Bowen to answer his pager, perking up as the registrar, his eyes as baggy as a Bassett hound's, sauntered towards her.

'Inspector,' he said. 'To what do I owe this unexpected pleasure?'

'Nothing special,' said West, smiling up at his gaunt but chiselled features, 'I was in the area so…'

'Not that old chestnut?'

'It's true. I've just come from the ICU, I had to check on Ferguson.'

'Oh aye, of course. And how is he?'

'Still out for the count but his breathing's improved. They reckon there's a chance they might be able to unplug him by this time tomorrow. Just thought you'd like to know, that's all.'

'Thanks,' said Bowen. 'I must admit, we get so many folk passing through here I tend not to keep an eye on them once they've left. If I did, I'd be an emotional wreck.'

'Well, if you don't mind me saying so, you look like one.'

'One of the benefits of shift work on the NHS. Still, it's good news about that Ferguson lad. You must be pleased.'

'Yeah, I am, but only because it means I won't be dealing with a murder inquiry and I might get some answers as to how he ended up in such a state. Have you actually eaten anything recently?'

'Of course,' said Bowen. 'A pot noodle and a couple of Mars bars.'

'You need feeding up,' said West hesitantly. 'Don't suppose you fancy an early lunch? I mean, if you've got time, that is.'

'Actually, I was going home to bed but now that you've mentioned it, aye, why not? Give me five minutes to change out of these and I'll be right with you.'

* * *

Having endured a tempestuous relationship with a self-centred toff who wore Savile Row suits followed by a doomed date with a Bohemian hipster who preferred to roll his jeans above the ankle to accentuate his hemp sandals, and a three day dalliance with an ex-colleague who considered combat fatigues ideal casualwear, when it came to matters of a sartorial nature West thought she'd seen it all until Dr Bowen, dressed in raggedy, oil-stained jeans, biker boots, and a vintage leather jacket returned to reception.

'Blimey,' she said, grinning approvingly, 'you look… different.'

'You've lost me.'

'Sorry, it's just that I was half-expecting to see you in a tweed jacket and a pair of brogues.'

'Not very practical on a bike,' said Bowen.

'Bike?'

'Aye. It's a Harley, a Fat Bob.'

'Sorry?'

'That's the name of the model, not the mechanic. Are you into bikes, Inspector?'

'Could be,' said West, raising her eyebrows. 'And the name's Charlotte, by the way. So, what do you fancy? Pasta? Pizza?'

'I know a wee place. Come with me.'

* * *

Though not as intimate as she'd have liked, West was willing to tolerate the open-plan seating, the harsh, fluorescent strip lights, and the din of the other diners deep in conversation, but having to queue with a tray in her hands behind a line of porters, nurses, and doctors was not what she'd expected.

'Where I come from,' she said as she tucked into a baked potato piled high with cheese and beans, 'when someone asks if you like hospital food, it's normally a veiled threat.'

'I'll let you into a secret,' said Bowen, 'this menu's designed to free up the beds quicker than a dose of laxatives. Whatever you do, stay away from the chicken korma.'

'So, long night, was it?'

'Just the usual,' said Bowen as he reached into his pocket, 'I'm used to it. Here, I got you a present.'

West, taken completely by surprise, could feel her cheeks flushing as she downed her cutlery and unfolded a slip of paper.

'Oh,' she said disappointedly. 'You shouldn't have.'

'Saves me the bother of emailing it. As you can see from the results, your man Ferguson was completely clean when he came in. No alcohol, no drugs. Of course, it's not conclusive, you'll have to wait for bloods to be sure.'

'Yeah, we will,' said West, 'thanks, anyway.'

'So,' said Bowen as he polished off his omelette, 'what does the rest of the weekend hold in store for you?'

'Nothing much apart from work, and with less than twelve hours remaining, it's hardly worth making plans.'

Bowen leaned back, sipped his milky tea and smiled.

'Have you ever ridden a motorbike?' he said.

'Nah, but I have been tempted. I was going to get one a few years back but I figured it'd only get in the way of my social life.'

'How's that?'

'Wouldn't do for a cop to get nicked for drink-driving, would it?'

'No, I see your point.'

'How about you?'

'Oh, I'll get my head down for a couple of hours, then take Ally for a blast along the coast.'

'Ally?' said West. 'I thought your bike was called Bob?'

'It is.'

West, looking as deflated as a burst balloon, stared at Bowen and forced a smile.

'I should be going,' she said. 'Lots to do.'

* * *

At just four and a half feet high and twelve feet long, the indisputable advantage of the Figaro was that, when parked amidst a row of average sized cars, it was completely imperceptible thereby allowing West – who thumped the steering with both hands while groaning through gritted teeth – to let off steam without drawing attention to herself before laughing at her own stupidity and calling Dougal for an update.

'Miss?' he said. 'Do you need for me for something?'

'What I need, Dougal, is a clown suit. I've just made a complete fool of myself.'

'Are you at the hospital?'

'Yes.'

'Doctor Bowen?'

'Might be.'

'Welcome to my world. What's up?'

'Just wanted to fill you in,' said West. 'They think they might be able to take Ferguson off life support tomorrow.'

'Oh, that is good news, miss, although it doesn't necessarily mean we'll get to talk to him.'

'No, I know, but at least it's a step in the right direction. What about you? How are you getting on?'

'Brilliantly,' said Dougal, 'have you got a minute?'

'Take as long as you like.'

'Okay, that bolt from the crossbow, it's made of ABS and manufactured by a company called MK. There's nowhere down here that sells that kind of thing, the nearest place is in Glasgow but I'll have to wait until tomorrow to ring them, then I can find out if they keep a log of their sales or if they've any regular customers, that kind of thing.'

'Okay, Dougal, nice one,' said West. 'That should cheer Jimbo up a bit and God knows it seems like he could do with it.'

'Not exactly embracing retirement, is he?'

'I couldn't have put it better myself.'

* * *

Salivating at the mouth-watering aroma of five and a half pounds of prime topside sizzling in the oven, West – already on her second glass – yelled down the hall as a surprisingly cheerful Munro returned from Carsethorn.

'Half an hour yet,' she said, 'you may as well grab yourself a drink.'

'I'll not need an invitation for that,' said Munro, smiling as he poured himself a large Balvenie.

'You're looking pleased with yourself. What's up?'

'Och, I've just had a rather pleasant surprise, that's all. You see, Charlie, I was expecting my new kitchen to be some flat-packed rubbish sent all the way from China but the gentlemen doing the work showed me a brochure and said I could have anything I wanted as the insurance company were going to foot the bill.'

'Well, that's great news,' said West. 'So, what are you going for? Some swanky state-of-the-art thing with a double oven, built-in microwave and a dishwasher?'

'Good heavens, no. I'm having solid oak and they're even going to lay some flagstones on the floor, but best of all, I shall have a smashing new oven just like the old one.'

'What? Are you mad?' said West. 'An opportunity like this and you want something that looks like it was built in the fifties?'

'Indeed I do,' said Munro, downing his whisky in favour of a glass of red. 'Trust me, Charlie, progress doesn't necessarily mean you're moving forward. No, no, I'm sticking with what I know.'

'Each to his own. So, you're happy, then?'

'Content, Charlie. Aye, that's the word. Content.'

Munro took a slug of wine, tucked a napkin into his collar and sat with his knife and fork grasped firmly in each hand like a couple of flag poles as West carved the joint and served up.

'You've excelled yourself, Charlie,' he said as she piled slice after slice onto his plate. 'Much appreciated.'

'Beans?'

Munro replied with a blank look of bewilderment on his face.

'You know, those long, green things called vegetables? Thought not. Just the spuds then?'

'Thanking you. So, how about you? How was your day?'

West topped up their glasses and raised her eyebrows.

'I've had better,' she said sheepishly.

'Och, I'm sorry to hear that. Did you not get to see this Ferguson chappie in the hospital?'

'Yup. They say there's a chance he might come round tomorrow, if he doesn't pop his clogs when they take him off life support.'

'And?'

'And what?'

'I'm not a fool, Charlie,' said Munro with a smirk. 'I've known you for far too long and there's one thing you'll never be – a poker player. You've not got the face for it.'

'Is it that obvious?'

'Unless I'm mistaken, I'd say this has something to do with somebody in the medical profession and if your track record's anything to go by, it's probably a pathologist.'

West took a large sip of wine, stared at Munro and smiled.

'Registrar,' she said.

'If you keep looking for it, Charlie, you'll never find it. One day it'll rear up and smack you in the face when you least expect it. Trust me.'

'Let's change the subject,' said West. 'I spoke to Dougal earlier, he thinks he might've found out where your crossbow bolt came from.'

'By jiminy, that was quick. How on earth does he do it?'

'Cos he's only half human. The other half's Apple.'

'Apple?'

'As in Mac.'

'I'm sure that means something,' said Munro with a gratified sigh. 'Now, remind me, did I purchase a pudding when I shopped for your groceries?'

'Yup,' said West as her phone rang. 'Get that will you, it's on speaker. Rhubarb crumble, coming up.'

'James Munro, gone but not forgotten. How can I help?'

'Alright, boss!' said Dougal. 'Do you want that on your headstone?'

'No, no, a simple "do not disturb" will suffice. Is it Charlie you're wanting?'

'I'm all ears,' said West. 'What's up?'

'I've been through Byrne's mobile, miss, he and this other fella spoke to each other four or five times the night he died. Going through his call history I'd say it must be a pal of his, name of Sean Jardine.'

'Then we should to speak to him,' said West. 'Have you got an address?'

'Not yet, miss,' said Dougal. 'I've got two hundred and thirty Jardines in Glasgow to get through, I'm just hoping there's not too many Seans.'

'Okay, well knowing you, that won't take long. What then?'

'Well, if I can find him tonight, then I thought I'd scoot up there first thing tomorrow and have a wee chat. I can call in on that place that sells the crossbows while I'm there.'

'Okay, no probs,' said West. 'Give me a buzz when you're done.'

* * *

'You've been gassing for ages, pal,' said Duncan. 'Have you been dialling that speaking clock, again?'

'Very funny,' said Dougal. 'I've been talking to West. What's so urgent?'

'I've just spoken with one of the lads stationed in Inverkip and have I got some news for you!'

'Do I need to sit down?'

'You need to take up drinking so you can celebrate.'

'I've an Irn-Bru in the fridge. Go on.'

'Okay, first of all, this fella, Bobby – he says there's a place near Shawlands that sells all that crossbow stuff…'

'Pollokshaws Road?'

'Aye, how did you…? Anyway, he also says there's a fella in the paintball crowd who takes it all a bit too seriously.'

'I'm not sure I understand.'

'He thinks he's a member of the SAS or something. Anyway, apparently he's into anything that doesn't need a firearms certificate; air pistols, rifles, BB guns… and crossbows.'

'That's super, Duncan, thanks. But how…?'

'Wait for it. His name's Sean Jardine and he works at the same bank as Alan Byrne.'

Chapter 6

Like so many start-ups seeking to emulate the success of the world's largest information technology company, Craig Ferguson's employers sought instant credibility by naming their company "iNET" and providing their workers with a crèche, a subsidised restaurant, a games room, and a chill-out area furnished entirely with bean bags all within the confines of a suitably modern, glass-fronted building in the fashionable Finnieston quarter of town.

Averse to traipsing into Cumnock for her weekly supplies let alone venturing into the city, Rona – raging at his impudent behaviour and furious that he'd not returned any of her calls – stormed through the doors where the achingly-hip girl on reception sporting a purple-dyed bob, a tattoo on her left shoulder, and enough piercings to make her a valuable asset to any scrap metal dealer, regarded her with a mild look of fear.

'Can I help?' she said nervously.

'Craig Ferguson, please.'

The young girl cocked her head to one side and frowned.

'Craig Ferguson?' she said, mystified. 'I'm sorry, but...'

'See here, missy,' said Rona, raising her voice, 'if he's asked you to cover for him, you can forget it. Tell him it's Rona and he's to get his arse down here, right now!'

'But…'

'I'll go myself, if I have to! Every floor. Top to bottom. Last chance.'

'But he doesn't work here anymore.'

Rona drew a breath as though she'd taken a body blow to the chest and gawped at the girl.

'Sorry?' she said.

'They let him go; must be five months now.'

'Five months?'

'Aye.'

'Well, where'd he go?'

'Search me. I've not seen him.'

'Home address? It's Minerva something, you must have his home address?'

'Aye, but I can't give you that,' said the girl, lowering her eyes. 'I'm sorry but it's…'

Rona leaned across the desk and glared at the cowering girl.

'Listen, hen,' she said, 'I'm not in the habit of pleading. I need to speak to him, now. It's urgent.'

Biting her bottom lip, the young girl thought for a moment, glanced over her shoulder, and relented.

'Okay,' she said as she tapped away at the keyboard, 'it's number twenty, Minerva Street. Flat one. But if anyone asks…'

* * *

Based on her own personal experience as a cash-strapped student searching for affordable digs she knew that a studio flat was nothing more than a glorified bedsit invariably located above a bookies or in some far-flung corner of a run-down tenement and definitely not the kind of accommodation associated with a four storey, Georgian terrace on a residential street with private parking and gated, communal gardens.

Convinced she'd arrived at the wrong address, Rona nonetheless buzzed the entry-phone and made her way up to the first floor where the door to the flat stood ajar. Easing it open, she called inside and was instantly embarrassed at having disturbed a distraught young lady in a padded puffer jacket with a wailing child in her arms.

'Oh, I was expecting somebody else,' said the woman, tugging at her ponytail. 'I'm waiting for my ride.'

'No, my fault,' said Rona, 'I'm in the wrong place, sorry for...'

'Who're you after?'

'No-one. Craig. I was looking for a Craig Ferguson.'

'You're not in the wrong place. This is Craig's home.'

'Really? Then you must be...?'

'Mary.'

'His sister?'

'His wife,' said Mary. 'And this is Jamie. His son.'

Feeling as though she'd been hit by a defibrillator on maximum charge, Rona stood rooted to the spot trying to catch her breath.

'Wife?' she said, her voice almost a whisper.

'Only until the divorce comes through, then that's me away. If it's any consolation, you're not the first. Craig's not one for bragging about his marital status.'

'Sorry,' said Rona, fearful of losing her composure. 'I should go.'

'No, you're alright. Was it something in particular you were wanting him for?'

'I just need a word,' said Rona, 'he's...'

'He's what? Stood you up? Done the dirty on you?'

'It doesn't matter.'

'I feel for you,' said Mary. 'A word of advice, next time you need him, try looking under a rock.'

'Aye. I will. Are you okay? You're looking a bit peaky.'

'I just need to get to the hospital, that's all.'

'The hospital? And there's me holding you up. Is it the bairn?'

'No, we're both fine. As it happens, it's Craig we're off to see…'

'Craig?'

'…he's landed himself in a spot of bother. Some fella knocked the crap out of him on Friday night.'

'Friday? Are you joking me?'

'I wish I was. I just hope he's not dead, I'm going to take that bawbag for every penny he's got.'

'Where is he? Glasgow Royal?'

'No,' said Mary. 'Ayr. He's probably got some tart hidden away down there.'

'Aye,' said Rona, lowering her eyes. 'Probably. Listen, do you… I mean, can I give you a lift? I'm heading that way and my car's just around the corner.'

'Thanks, but my brother's taking us, he should be here by… oh, speak of the devil, grab my bag would you.'

The short, blond-haired, thirty-seven year old who looked as though he'd swallowed a stack of steroids before squeezing himself into a suit two sizes too small, proffered a podgy hand and eyed Rona like a stalker.

'Pleased to meet you,' he said with a twisted grin.

* * *

In a bid to make an impression on West which would consign his hitherto erratic and at times unprofessional behaviour to the history books, Duncan – having risen early enough to reach his desk by 7 a.m. – looked as though he'd spent the night cuddling a kebab on a park bench in the Cairngorms.

'Blimey, you look rough,' said West, smiling as she breezed through the door.

'Nice to see you, too,' said Duncan, rubbing his bloodshot eyes.

'What are you up to?'

'I'm trying to figure out where Byrne could've laid his hands on that Buprenorphine. Five hours I've been at it and nothing so far. Where is everyone?'

'Dougal's in Glasgow and I got bogged down with the forensics report on Craig Ferguson's motor.'

'Anything?'

'Not a sausage,' said West, 'speaking of which, I got lunch on the way in.'

'Thanks very much. Is the chief not with you?'

'Nope. You're forgetting, he's not one of us anymore.'

'Oh, aye, that's right,' said Duncan, unwrapping a toastie. 'Christ, he's like a part of the furniture, though. I'm not sure I can get used to him not being around.'

'You don't have to, not yet. He's gone shopping, he'll be here soon.'

'The chief? Shopping?'

'I know,' said West. 'Bonkers, isn't it?

'What's he after?'

'Plants, I think, for the garden. And a toaster, and a kettle.'

'Department store, then.'

'I wouldn't count on it. Knowing Jimbo, he's probably rummaging round a junk shop looking for something that was built fifty years ago.'

'Nothing wrong with recycling, I suppose,' said Duncan as he ruffled his unruly hair. 'Tea?'

'Yes, please. So, what's the deal with Alan Byrne?'

'He's giving me a headache.'

'Then consider me your aspirin.'

'Okay,' said Duncan, heaving a sigh. 'I've been on to his GP. He has a check-up every year, regular as clockwork, and he's as fit as a fiddle, doesn't even get so much as a sniffle. He's not a heavy drinker and he's no history of substance abuse, so, no referral to rehab.'

West leaned back in her chair and, gathering her thoughts, stared pensively at the ceiling as she sipped her tea.

'Any biscuits?' she said.

'Aye. Ginger nuts, in the tin.'

'What about bloods?'

'Apart from the 'prenorphine and a wee drop of alcohol, nothing. And pathology say his insides were like a well-oiled machine. Everything was in good working order.'

'Okay, then that leaves one of two possible options: either it was his first time and he blew it by...'

'No, no, no,' said Duncan. 'I can't buy that, miss, sorry. Not with Buprenorphine. Like I say, it's not like scoring weed or a couple of lines, this stuff is hard to come by.'

'Then that leaves the second option which is, somebody gave it to him. Either they administered it forcibly or he took it unwittingly.'

'Aye, that's possible, I suppose.'

'Good, so the question is how? This Buprenorphine, does it come in tablet form or is it a liquid?'

'Both.'

'And is it odourless or tasteless? I mean, could it be slipped into a drink or a meal?'

'It could, aye.'

'And you're absolutely sure you can't just get it off the internet? Get it shipped over from the States or somewhere?'

'Oh, you can never be one hundred per cent, miss, but I doubt it.'

'Okay then,' said West as she dunked a biscuit into her tea, 'in that case, whoever topped him must have had easy access to it. What about his personal life? Relationships?'

'Single. From what I can gather, the only thing he was in love with was the gym.'

'Then you need to find out who he dated or even slept with in the last six months, including one-night stands.'

'Roger that.'

'In particular, anyone who works in rehab, or as a nurse or a doctor, even a receptionist at a surgery.'

'On it.'

'And you could do worse than starting with that mate of his, that Jardine bloke.'

'Jardine?' said Duncan. 'Of course! You do know he works at the same bank as Byrne?'

'You're kidding?'

'No, I found out last night. I told Dougal.'

'Well, it looks like the two of them were mates, after all. Jardine rang Byrne at least half a dozen times the night he died.'

'You don't suppose he could've…'

'Who knows. Give Dougal a shout, he's up there now. See if he's spoken to him yet.'

* * *

With a look that belied his inherent hatred of shopping, Munro – grinning like a grandad who'd spent his entire pension on Christmas gifts for his grandchildren – ambled into the office and placed two large carrier bags on the desk.

'This,' he said, smiling smugly as he held aloft a box featuring a photo of a chrome-plated toaster, 'is the jewel in the crown of appliances. Not only does it have a timer but with these wee racks, you can pop an entire sandwich in there! It'll even melt the cheese.'

'Shame you weren't here half an hour ago, chief,' said Duncan, 'we could've given it a test run.'

'There's always tomorrow, laddie. As my kitchen's not fit for purpose, we may as well make use of it.'

'Did you get a kettle that also boils eggs?' said West.

'I did not, Charlie. But I did get one that's capable of inflicting a serious head injury. So, what's occurring? Is there anything I can help you with?'

'Nah, not right now,' said West. 'Anyway, I thought you were up to your elbows with Billy the Goat?'

'I am indeed,' said Munro, 'but we appear to have reached an impasse in the inquiry. I'm waiting to hear from young Dougal about the bolt.'

'It's your lucky day, chief,' said Duncan. 'He's up there, now.'

'What did he say?' said West. 'Has he spoken to Jardine?'

'No, he missed him. He was only in for an hour or so then had to leave. Some sort of family crisis or something.'

'Is that sandwich for me?' said Munro.

'Yup, all yours,' said West, interrupted by the ring of her phone, 'sausage and brown sauce. DI West, who's this?'

'Sorry for troubling you,' came a trembling voice, 'but it's the old fella I'm wanting, Mr Munro, is it?'

'James Munro?'

'Aye, that's him. I don't have his number, this one was on the card he gave me. It's Rona Macallan.'

'The goat lady?'

'Aye, that's me.'

'Hold on,' said West as she handed the phone to Munro.

'Miss Macallan, how are you?'

'Not good, Mr Munro. Not good at all. I need you here. I was going to call the police but I thought it best I...'

'Will you calm yourself, Miss Macallan!' said Munro tersely. 'Whatever is the matter?'

'There's a fella been harassing me. Threatening me.'

'Is he there now?'

'No, he's just left. I was away in Glasgow, see, and...'

'By jiminy, Miss Macallan! Take a deep breath! Now, one step at a time, tell me what's happened.'

'Sorry. I went to see Craig...'

'Who's Craig?'

'Craig Ferguson, he's my... well, he was my...'

'Hold it right there,' said Munro as he passed the phone to West, 'Charlie, put this infernal device on speaker, you need to hear this. Apologies, Miss Macallan. Now, what's all this about Craig Ferguson?'

West's ears pricked up at the mention of his name.

'He and I were in a relationship,' said Rona.

'Can you be more specific?' said West.

'We met a few months ago but he lives miles away, so he comes to me on a Friday and stops the weekend. Last Friday he'd barely got through the door but when I told him about Esme he took off like a shot. I've not heard from him since, so I went to his house.'

'In Glasgow?'

'Aye. Anyway, it turns out he's married, see, and his wife was on her way to the hospital because she said he'd had some kind of accident. Her brother was giving her a lift.'

'Did you go with them?'

'I showed them the way.'

'And did you see Craig?'

'No, they said he wasn't allowed visitors so I left my number and came home.'

'Okay,' said West, 'and then?'

'I'm not long indoors and her brother, the fella who gave her a lift, pulls up outside.'

'So, he followed you?'

'Right enough,' said Rona. 'And he's scary looking, you know, like he's not right in the head. Then he starts shouting at me and waving his arms and...'

'What was he shouting?' said West.

'I couldn't hear. I locked the door and ran upstairs. Why would he do that? I've not met the man before, why would he threaten me?'

'I've no idea,' said Munro as he fastened his coat, 'but I'm on my way over. You stay put and dinnae answer the door to anyone. This fella, did you get a name? Did he introduce himself?'

'Aye, his name's Sean. Sean Jardine.'

A momentary silence filled the air as West, raising her hand to prevent anyone from speaking, locked eyes with Duncan.

'Miss Macallan,' she said sternly, 'listen to me, this is important. Do you remember what car he was driving?'

'No, my head's all over the shop. Let me think. It was blue, I think. Aye, dark blue. And sporty. A BMW.'

'Duncan,' said West as she hung up the phone, 'get yourself over to the hospital, speak to Ferguson's wife and find out where Jardine lives.'

'Roger that, miss.'

'And ask her if she knows his car reg, if she doesn't, then call Dougal, tell him to get his arse back to the bank; if they've got on-site parking then they should have his details.'

Chapter 7

Not quite the picture of inconsolable grief he was expecting, Mary Ferguson – seated outside a room in the ICU with a bairn on her lap, her coat on the floor, and a look of fury on her face – scowled at Duncan as he ambled towards her.

'Mrs Ferguson?' he said, raising a smile as he flashed his warrant card. 'DC Reid, can I trouble you for a moment?'

'Oh, here we go,' said Mary. 'What?'

'It's about your brother, Sean.'

'Sean? What are you wanting him for? Should you not be looking for the bampot who did this to Craig?'

'We are,' said Duncan, 'and before you go off on one, we've been working on it all weekend and my colleagues have been here every day to check on him.'

'Oh, I see,' said Mary shamefully. 'Well, that's alright then.'

'Your brother's car, would you happen to know the registration number?'

'Don't be daft! Why would I…'

'Then, I need his home address.'

'What for?'

'I'll not ask again, Mrs Ferguson. Address, please.'

'Miller Street. Sixty-four. Top floor.'

'I'll be right back.'

* * *

Safely out of earshot, Duncan pulled out his phone, cursing as he paced back and forth waiting for an answer.

'At last!' he said. 'Dougal, where are you?'

'Pollokshaws Road.'

'Are you driving?'

'No, I'm pulled up.'

'Okay, you'll not believe this but that Craig Ferguson fella; he's been having it away with the goat lady.'

'Rona Macallan? Well, well. Talk about six degrees of separation.'

'Aye, not only that, he's married too, but here's the best bit: his brother-in-law is Sean Jardine.'

'Jardine?' said Dougal. 'Jeez-oh, at last things are getting interesting.'

'You're not wrong, there, pal. Get this: Jardine dropped Mary Ferguson at the hospital this morning then for some reason he headed straight for Rona Macallan's and started threatening her.'

'Is that so? Well, I suppose if he knows his sister's husband has been playing around, then maybe he's just looking out for her.'

'Maybe.'

'Either way,' said Dougal, 'we should bring him in as soon as possible.'

'That's what Westy said. She reckons we've enough to have him for trespass and threatening behaviour, so that'll give us a chance to question him about Byrne, and Macallan too.'

'Do we know where he is?'

'No,' said Duncan, 'we know he's driving a dark blue BMW but we've not got any details. Listen, do they have secure parking at that bank of his?'

'They do. I used it myself.'

'Magic. She wants you back there.'

'Why?'

'Because we've not got time to go back the office and we can't run a trace through DVLA without the registration.'

'Okay,' said Dougal. 'Leave it with me and I'll get it circulated.'

'Then she wants you to check on his flat in case he's gone back home. Will I text you the address?'

'No need, I already have it – Miller Street.'

'Aye, Miller Street,' said Duncan. 'Now, why does that sound so familiar?'

'It's the same address as Alan Byrne, you dafty. Same address.'

* * *

Trying his best to appear sympathetic, Duncan, head hung low, shuffled back along the corridor with his hands in his pockets and spoke softly.

'Sorry, Mrs Ferguson,' he said. 'I had to make a call. Have you seen him yet? Craig?'

'I have not,' said Mary, 'and it doesn't look as if I will, either. Not for a while yet.'

'Well, can I fetch you something? A tea, maybe? Or a blanket for the bairn?'

'No. What you can fetch me is something that'll bring that good-for-nothing husband of mine back to the land of the living.'

'Look,' said Duncan, 'I'm no expert, and I know folk have different ways of coping with grief but if you don't mind saying so, you seem more angry than upset.'

'Angry is not the word,' said Mary. 'I'm fizzing! Whoever did this obviously doesn't realise I've a bairn to look after and if Craig dies then that's me humped. What'll I do for money then?'

'Aye, fair point. So, you really have no idea who might be responsible for this? I mean, is there anyone Craig might've rubbed up the wrong way?'

'No chance. Any sign of trouble and he's away on his toes.'

'What about his pals? Anyone he might've upset?'

'He doesn't get out enough to have any pals.'

'Work colleagues?'

Mary turned to Duncan and raised her eyebrows, a sarcastic smile accentuating the premature wrinkles on her pale, drawn face.

'Craig's not had a job in months,' she said. 'He was sacked.'

'Oh, that's too bad,' said Duncan, shaking he head. 'Cutbacks was it? The economy, right?'

'Gross misconduct. Inappropriate behaviour.'

Trying not to look too surprised, Duncan squatted down beside her and casually rubbed his chin.

'I don't suppose you'd like to tell me what it is he did, exactly?'

'No. I would not. It's too embarrassing.'

'Then, I'll not ask again. Listen, about your brother, Mrs Ferguson, he was here earlier, right?'

'Aye, he was. He gave me a lift.'

'He gave you a lift all the way from Glasgow and didn't hang around to keep you company?'

'No,' said Mary, 'he said he had things to do. He's not one for compassion, is Sean.'

'Would you happen to know if he's friendly with a lady called Rona Macallan?'

'Macallan? You mean the woman who came to my house?'

'Aye. That's her.'

'Well, how could he know her? They've only just met, on my doorstep, if you please.'

'I'm just covering all the bases, Mrs Ferguson. That's all.'

Duncan hauled himself to his feet, his eyes drawn to the bruise-like blemishes on Mary's bony, bare arms, and buttoned his coat.

'Thanks for your help,' he said. 'I've kept you long enough.'

'Cheery-bye.'

'Just one thing: are you clean, now?'

'You what?'

'Are you clean? Or are you still using?'

'Excuse me?'

'I'm not blind, Mrs Ferguson.'

'I'm on a programme,' said Mary indignantly.

'Glad to hear it. Where do you go?'

'What's it to you?'

'I said where do you go?'

'The Crisis Centre. West Street.'

'And is Craig into this junk as well?'

'No,' said Mary. 'That's not him, he'll not even take a coffee; he's that soft.'

'How about Sean? I hear it's all the rage with these city whizz-kids.'

'Not that meathead, he's other ways of getting his kicks.'

'Such as?'

'He likes to play the hard-man.'

'How so?' said Duncan. 'You mean he's violent?'

'He can be. He likes looking for trouble.'

'So, does he deliberately get himself into situations where things might kick-off?'

'Aye,' said Mary, her shoulders slumping as she sighed, 'but the thing about Sean is, he'll only pummel someone if he knows they'll not fight back. Small man syndrome, I think they call it.'

'And does he do this often?'

'Not as much as he used to. Not since he got that thing going with his pal.'

'What pal?'

'Alan something or other.'

'Byrne?'

'Aye, that's him.'

'So, what's this thing they've got going?'

'You'd best ask him.'

'I will,' said Duncan, 'when we find him. In the meantime, I'm asking you.'

Mary gazed blankly at the opposite wall as she weighed up the pros and cons of divulging details of her brother's exploits before heaving another weary sigh.

'Loans,' she said. 'Money-lending. They're a couple of sharks.'

'Really? So, they have plenty of cash to splash around?'

'Wake up, Constable. They're bankers. They earn more sitting on the toilet than I'd earn in ten years. Sean's idea of disposable income is not the same as normal folk.'

'Go on.'

'So, he lends it to what he calls *the needy*. Not his own family, mind, just the schemes and the junkies.'

'That's very philanthropic of him. And he gets off on that?'

'No,' said Mary, 'he gets off on putting them through the mincer when they can't make the repayments. And when I say "mincer", I'm not far off the mark. I'd watch out if I were you.'

'And why's that?'

'They've both got letters after their names – GBH.'

'Are you sure?'

'Oh, aye. Positive. They're nutters.'

* * *

Unsettled by the barrage of verbal abuse hurled at her by an irate Jardine, Rona – concerned that he might return at any moment – grabbed the poker from the fire and dashed upstairs where, hiding behind the net curtains, she waited anxiously until the sight of an ageing Peugeot bumping up the pot-holed drive brought her bounding down the stairs.

'Am I glad to see you!' she said, smiling with relief as she flung open the door. 'It's like I said, I'm not long home when…'

'Wheesht!' said Munro as he raised his hands. 'Let's not have a rerun of our conversation earlier, Miss Macallan. Now, first things first: this is Detective Inspector Charlotte West.'

'Sorry,' said Rona. 'I'm getting ahead of myself. We spoke earlier, did we not?'

'Yup, we sure did,' said West as she began texting on her phone. 'Before we go any further, can you give us a description of this Jardine bloke? I want to send it to my team as soon as possible.'

'Aye, easy. He's a short-arse – five-four, five-five. Brown eyes, blondish hair. Freckles.'

'Very good,' said Munro. 'Age?'

'Oh, mid-thirties, I'd say. And he's stocky, looks like he's made out of Lego.'

'That's very observant of you.'

'Well, you have to be, don't you? Observant, I mean. Especially when you've got livestock to look after. Will we go inside?'

* * *

With breakfast a distant memory, West eagerly accepted the offer of a mug of tea and several slices of crusty, homemade bread smothered with goats' cheese before proceeding to quiz Rona at length about her encounter with Jardine under the watchful eye of Munro – who sat sipping his brew like an adjudicator at a chess match – before concluding, somewhat disappointingly, that there was no obvious reason for Jardine's minatory behaviour nor any apparent connection with her errant boyfriend.

Declining an invitation to meet the chickens and pet the ponies, she remained indoors and watched from the window as Rona escorted Munro to the far side of the meadow where a simple wooden cross marked the spot where Esme had been laid to rest, leaving her with nothing but the monotonous tick-tock of a wall clock for company.

'Duncan!' she said as she whipped her phone from her hip. 'It's like a flipping morgue here. Have you spoken to Craig's wife?'

'I have,' said Duncan. 'It's all sorted. Dougal's on his way to the bank as we speak, then he's off to Jardine's flat. You'll like this; guess where he lives.'

'Oh, I haven't got time for games, Duncan, just tell me.'

'Miller Street. He's got an apartment right next door to Alan Byrne.'

'Byrne? Bosom buddies, eh?'

'They'd have to be. Apart from working together, they've both been running some kind of loan racket.'

'Are you serious?'

'I kid you not, miss. I got it straight from the horse's mouth. Almost. They loan out cash to desperate neds, then batter them black and blue if they default on the repayments.'

'What? Well, why the hell would anyone do that?'

'They're unhinged,' said Duncan. 'According to Mary Ferguson they've both got form – GBH.'

'Well, why didn't that come up when you ran a check on Byrne?'

'I've no idea. I suppose if it was a while back then maybe the conviction's spent.'

'Shouldn't make any difference. Check it again,' said West. 'I want to know exactly where and when they were sentenced. Got that?'

'Miss.'

'Anything else?'

70

'Aye, there is,' said Duncan. 'Craig Ferguson; he's not had a job in months. He was dismissed for inappropriate behaviour.'

'You what? You mean, like sexual assault?'

'She wouldn't say, but we could find out if we have to.'

'No, not yet,' said West, 'let's keep that one up our sleeve for now. Hold on a mo', if Ferguson's out of work, then how is he paying the bills?'

'I'm not sure, miss. Savings, maybe?'

Assuming that West was employing the silent treatment as a sign of her disdain for the ludicrous suggestion that a young, married couple with a baby had enough savings to sustain them for five months or more, Duncan held his tongue and prepared himself for an ear-bashing.

'Miss?' he said sheepishly. 'Are you still there?'

'Yeah, sorry Duncan,' said West as she watched Munro amble across the meadow, 'just trying to get inside someone's head.'

'Come again?'

'Nothing. Listen. Craig Ferguson; long-term unemployed, right?'

'Aye, apparently.'

'He's got a wife and a child to support plus a mortgage to pay, and yet he's running around in a brand new motor. How does that work? I mean, are they claiming any benefits?'

'Even if they were, it wouldn't be enough to pay for all of that.'

'Then where's the dosh coming from?'

'Like I said, savings?'

'Don't be silly.'

'Okay,' said Duncan, 'then maybe it's severance pay? Maybe he got some kind of pay-off?'

'Or maybe,' said West, 'he knew exactly what his brother-in-law was up to and he tapped him for a loan.'

'Could be, but wouldn't Mary Ferguson know about that?'

'Why would she? Look, you just said Jardine likes to batter his clients black and blue, right?'

'Aye, that's what she said.'

'So, Craig loses his job and gets a loan off Jardine, but when he can't repay it, Jardine collars him and puts him in the ICU.'

'Oh, I'm not sure, miss,' said Duncan. 'His own brother-in-law?'

'You don't know much about families, do you, Duncan? Did Mary Ferguson mention anything about her relationship with her brother?'

'As a matter of fact, she did. They don't get along, at all.'

'Well, then. There you go.'

'And she and Craig are getting a divorce.'

'Bingo.'

'There something else,' said Duncan. 'She's a drug addict. Well, an ex-addict.'

'You have got to be kidding! Why didn't you say so earlier?'

'With all due respect, miss, I've only just found out! She's on a programme at the Crisis Centre in Glasgow.'

'Even better,' said West as she gazed from the kitchen window, her eyes boring into Munro as he and Rona headed towards the house. 'What's she on? Methadone?'

'I imagine so,' said Duncan. 'It's the opioid of choice for recovering junkies.'

'But it could be 'prenorphine?'

'Could be.'

'Okay,' said West, frowning as her mind went into overdrive, 'let's rejig that scenario. Craig Ferguson loses his job, right? So, he gets a loan off Byrne and Jardine, then when he realises he can't repay it, he turns to his wife for help. She knows her brother wouldn't piss on her if she was on fire so she swipes some 'prenorphine from the clinic and between them they get rid of Byrne. Jardine finds out and knocks the living daylights of Craig.'

'I'm not sure my brain was built to handle so much information, miss. It's possible, I'll give you that, but…'

'But what?'

'But surely there's an easier way of doing it?'

'There is,' said West, 'but this didn't cost them anything and what's more, it just looks like an overdose, right?'

'Okay, but then why has Jardine got it in for Rona Macallan?'

'Easy,' said West. 'Jardine knows his sister hasn't got two pennies to rub together so there's no way he'd get his money back from her, but if he knew Craig was having an affair with Rona Macallan…'

'Of course!' said Duncan. 'He'd go after her for the cash. So, what now? Will I head back to the office?'

'Yes,' said West, 'as quick as you can. I want a list of any convictions Byrne and Jardine have got, spent or otherwise, and I want you to contact the rehab place you mentioned and find out if they've had any break-ins, robberies, or any stock go missing in the past couple of weeks.'

'By stock, you mean Buprenorphine?'

'That's exactly what I mean. And if they have, see if it coincides with any of Mary Ferguson's appointments.'

'Roger that. Where will you be?'

'I'm going to drag Jimbo down the hospital and have another word with her.'

* * *

Saddled with living out of a suitcase until the restoration work on his house was complete and, thanks to his retirement, prohibited from leading any kind of official investigation, an unsettled Munro – not given to bouts of melancholy – couldn't help but feel a pang of jealousy as he watched the goats and the chickens nibbling on grass and grain burdened with nothing more than the simple task of sating their appetites.

He stood in the doorway and mustered a half-hearted smile as West, a hairgrip clenched between her teeth, pinned her tumbling brown locks atop her head.

'Blimey,' she said, perturbed by his doleful expression, 'you alright? You look like you've just run over a koala bear.'

'Aye,' said Munro. 'I'm fine, lassie. It's a lovely cross Miss Macallan's made for the grave. Fashioned from birch, no less. If my Jean didnae have a headstone, I'd take her one of those.'

'Cheerful as ever,' said West, zipping her coat. 'Where is she?'

'Putting the goats in the pen, just in case. She'll be along in a minute or two.'

'Can't hang around, Jimbo, we'll say our goodbyes on the way out.'

'For heaven's sake, Charlie, why the rush?'

'We need to have a word with Mary Ferguson.'

'We?'

'Yeah, I could do with the company.'

'No, no, you're on your own, Charlie. I've something I must attend to. I'll drop you there and Duncan can pick you up.'

'Don't be daft, it won't take long.'

'Oh, no,' said Rona, wiping her feet on the mat, 'don't tell me you're off already?'

'Sorry, Miss Macallan,' said West, 'duty calls, as they say.'

'Oh well, I suppose if you must. It's just that…'

'Miss Macallan,' said Munro, 'there's no need to fret. We're already looking for this Jardine fellow and I can assure you there's very little chance he'll be back. Take yourself indoors and lock the door. You'll be fine, I promise you. Just fine.'

Chapter 8

With the autumn harvest almost over, the desolate fields flanking the road to Ayr – overshadowed by an ominous raft of thunderous grey clouds laden with the threat of a torrential downpour – looked bleaker than normal.

Munro, his right hand on the wheel, the left on the gearstick, and his mind elsewhere, said nothing as the wipers glided effortlessly across the rain-spattered windscreen.

'You're quiet, Jimbo,' said West. 'Something up?'

'No, no. I'm just… thinking.'

'About what?'

Munro hesitated and cast a sideways glance at West.

'The house,' he said. 'Aye, that's it. The house.'

'Yeah, must be a pain in the backside but these things take time. If you start rushing them, they'll only cock it up.'

'Quite right, Charlie. Good things come to those who wait.'

'Exactly.'

'But sometimes that good thing can be somewhat disappointing.'

'How d'you mean?'

'Ignore me,' said Munro. 'I'm havering.'

'Well, it goes without saying you can crash at mine for as long as you like, you know that, don't you?'

'I do indeed, lassie. And for that, I'm grateful. Believe me.'

'No sweat,' said West, smiling. 'Oops, hold on, phone call. Dougal, did you get my text about Jardine?'

'Aye, miss. I did. I also got a mugshot from security, the one he uses on his pass. I've circulated it with details of his car, everyone's on the lookout for it.'

'Nice one.'

'And there's no-one at his flat. I did wait a while but no joy. Will I get Glasgow to give the door a nudge?'

'God, no,' said West. 'Hang fire on that, we can't go knocking his door down. Not yet.'

'Okay,' said Dougal, 'in that case I'm heading back to the office. Oh, by the way, I've some news on that bolt from the crossbow, too.'

'Well, dinnae keep it to yourself,' said Munro. 'Speak up.'

'Boss! I didn't realise you were there! It's not good, I'm afraid. They're ten a penny…'

'Cheap at half the price.'

'…and they're not restricted. A wean could buy them.'

'Well, at least you tried, Dougal. It's much appreciated.'

'Let's not give up just yet, boss. Are you coming in later?'

'Aye, just as soon as Charlie's had a word with this Ferguson lassie. Give us an hour or so.'

* * *

Content to wait in the warmth of the car while she attended to business, Munro watched as West, seemingly impervious to the worsening deluge, strolled casually across the car park with her hands in her pockets, before reaching for his phone.

'James!' boomed DCI Elliot. 'This is a surprise! How the devil are you? Taking a break from all that painting and decorating, I imagine?'

'Actually, I'm outside the hospital.'

'Nothing serious, I hope?'

'No, no. I'm waiting for Charlie.'

'Charlie? Is she okay?'

'Aye, we're all okay!' said Munro impatiently. 'Listen, can you spare a few minutes? I need a wee word.'

'Sorry James, but I'm on my way out.'

'By jiminy, George, you've turned clock-watching into an art form.'

'Now, now, James,' said Elliot as he stood to leave. 'As it happens, Mrs Elliot has prepared something special for my supper.'

'Oh, aye?'

'Beef Wellington.'

'Well, I wouldn't want to sour a beautiful relationship,' said Munro, glibly. 'After all, you and your belly have known each other a long time.'

'Do I detect a hint of sarcasm?'

'Sarcasm? Come, come, George, you know me better than that.'

'Well, what's so important that it can't wait until the morning?'

'I need to speak to you about... about re-engagement.'

'Good grief!' said Elliot, falling to his seat. 'It's not been a week since you retired! What's going on?'

'I'm dying of boredom.'

'James. Look. I'd have you back at the drop of a hat, but re-engagement? That could take weeks, and it's not without its complications, either. Like your pension for a start.'

'I'm aware of that.'

'And you know you can't just walk back into your old job, it'll be desk duties or... or you'd have to be a special.'

'Och, well,' said Munro. 'Plan B it is, then.'

'Plan B?'

'How are your staffing levels, George?'

'You know full well, James. Dire.'

'Then would you not be happy to enlist the services of a civilian volunteer?'

'A what?'

'There's already a couple in the office.'

'Aye, there are!' said Elliot, flabbergasted at the suggestion. 'But they're on reception, James! Filing duties and the like! To be honest, I'm not even sure there is such a thing as volunteer DI.'

'Well, think of me as a consultant, then. Or an advisor. Listen, George, the fact of the matter is, if I dinnae start doing something productive soon, then that's the end. That's me away.'

'Where to? Back to Carsethorn?'

'To an early grave.'

Munro allowed himself a wry smile as the ensuing silence indicated things were swinging in his favour.

'You do realise,' said Elliot, 'that as a volunteer there'll be no salary? You'll not get a bean for your efforts, you know that?'

'I'll not need a salary, George.'

'And there'll be no rank, so you'll not be able to head-up an inquiry, you'll never be an SIO.'

'Aye. I know.'

'And it's Charlie you'll have to answer to. There'll be none of this running off and doing your own thing.'

'Understood.'

'Okay,' said Elliot, smiling at the prospect of Munro returning to the fold. 'I'll look into it.'

'When?'

'Tomorrow. There's no guarantees mind, not at this stage, but if it's doable, then you're in. With one proviso.'

'And what would that be?'

'Expenses.'

'Och, I'll not be troubling you with that, George.'

'Oh, but you will, James. I insist.'

* * *

Wishing she'd worn a sou'wester rather than her hoodless jacket, a sodden West jumped in the front seat, hastily unpinned her hair and shook her head like a lively Labrador after a satisfying dip in a lake, showering a grinning Munro in the process.

'What are you looking so happy about?' she said.

'Och, you'll find out soon enough, lassie. You'll find out soon enough.'

'I'm getting worried about you and your mood swings, you're acting like a schizo.'

'How'd you get on?'

'I'm not sure,' said West as she slipped off her coat and buckled up. 'She seems straight-up. I just find it hard to believe that anyone in her position could be so trusting... no, so naïve, about her finances.'

'How so?'

'Well, she doesn't worry about money, so she claims, she leaves all that to Craig and so far as she knows, apart from the mortgage, they, or rather Craig, don't have any loans or debts, no maxed-out credit cards and they definitely don't claim benefits. And to top it all, he bungs a few hundred quid into her account every month. And when I said it seemed a bit odd bearing in mind that her husband's been unemployed for yonks, she just stared at me like... like I'd asked her if she knew what DNA was.'

'Deoxyribonucleic acid.'

'Is it really?'

'So, he's no other credit cards stashed away? No crafty savings account he's kept hidden to himself?'

'Nope. Well, not according to her.'

'Then, if I were you,' said Munro, 'considering the current state of his health, I'd do some more checking before he slips this mortal coil, and if he comes up clean, then it begs the question: where's the cash coming from?'

'Exactly,' said West, 'and you'll be pleased to know, I've been giving that some serious thought.'

'Careful, Charlie, the brain's a delicate organ, if you work it too hard you'll be needing a lie down.'

'What I'm needing is food. I'm flipping famished.'

'Aye, well, it is supper time, I'll grant you that. Let's drop by the office first and you can tell me your theory on the way.'

* * *

With an unseasonably dark sky depriving them of daylight and neither of them motivated enough to reach for the light switch, Duncan and Dougal sat silently in the gloom, the former scribbling furiously on a notepad like a scholar revising for an exam whilst Dougal pounded the keyboard manipulating images from the digital camera wired to his computer, both oblivious to West's request for a steaming cuppa and a teacake.

'Blimey,' she said with a huff, 'if this is what real police work is like, I'm going back to waitressing.'

'The food would never make it to the table,' said Munro. 'Dougal, what's the story?'

'Remember I said don't give up, boss?'

'Did you?'

'Take a look at this.'

Munro stood behind Dougal, hands clasped behind his back, and stared, nonplussed, at what appeared to be a blank screen.

'A black cat in a coal cellar?' he said, shrugging his shoulders.

'It's a shaft, boss. The shaft of the bolt that killed the goat.'

'Is that so?'

'Aye, see here,' said Dougal as he traced his index finger across the screen, 'I noticed this when I was showing it to the fella in the shop. At first I thought it was a manufacturing defect but the fella disputed it and now I see why: it's a scratch. Dead straight, very fine, and not too deep.'

Munro, already one step ahead, glanced across at West and smiled.

'And what conclusions have you drawn from this exercise in forensic analysis, Dougal?'

'Well, boss, I reckon…'

'You reckon the pistol bow that fired this bolt has an imperfection on the barrel.'

'Aye! Exactly! Not much, a wee burr maybe. It might not even be visible to the naked eye but it's enough to do this.'

'Meaning?'

'Meaning, boss,' said Dougal with a satisfied grin, 'that if we find the owner of the bow, then we'll probably have the goat killer, too.'

'Hold on,' said West. 'I don't quite follow, I mean, if what you say is true then wouldn't the scratch be a spiral? Don't those things spin when they're fired? Like a bullet?'

'They do indeed, lassie,' said Munro, holding up the bolt, 'in flight. But see here, the bolt's fletched, and this wee tail sits in a channel in the barrel, so when fired, the scratch would be perfectly straight.'

'That's me told. Okay, so based on what Mary Ferguson and Rona Macallan's told us, the obvious culprit has to be Jardine. If he doesn't turn up soon I think we'll have to let ourselves in to his flat.'

'Excuse me for interrupting,' said Duncan, waving his notepad, 'but if you lot have finished interviewing David Bailey, there, I've something you might be interested in. It's nothing to do with animals I'm afraid but it is linked to a murder investigation and a case of GBH.'

'Hark at you, Poirot,' said West. 'Come on then, let's have it.'

'Okay, I've been following up your theory, miss, that Mary Ferguson might have got her hands on the 'prenorphine from the clinic she attends.'

'This should be interesting.'

'They've not had any robberies or break-ins as such but there was an incident just a couple of weeks ago. Now, it may just be circumstantial but a member of staff was treating a client and took a pack of 'prenorphine from the cupboard but it was empty.'

'Sounds promising.'

'Obviously they logged it and reported it to the suppliers but…'

'Don't blow me out of the water, Duncan.'

'…but here's the thing: the only other person on 'prenorphine that day was Mary Ferguson and her appointment was at nine-fifteen. The empty pack was discovered at four pm.'

'Clever cow!' said West. 'Instead of taking the whole pack, she simply swiped the contents!'

'Aye. Possibly. But for that to happen, the counsellor would've had to have the left room for a minute or two; there's no way she'd have been able to do it otherwise.'

'Cameras,' said Munro. 'It's a rehab clinic, they'll have more cameras than Twentieth Century Fox.'

'Ahead of you, there, chief. I've requested all their footage from eight-thirty am to ten am.'

'Good for you, laddie. Aye, in fact, good work all round. Well, if that concludes business for the day I see no reason to linger any longer. Charlie, time for a wee quiz before we go. If I said to you, "well done", what would you say?'

'Sirloin,' said West with a smirk.

'And if I said, "Cabernet Franc", what would you say?'

'I'd say stop talking gibberish and get your skates on.'

* * *

Unable to decide whether she was blessed with the driving skills of Emerson Fittipaldi or simply harboured a desire to meet her maker, Munro – keeping his distance – winced as he watched the speeding Figaro weave its way through the rain-soaked streets before grinding to a halt outside the flat where a jubilant West waved childishly as she leapt from the car and dashed inside.

Acting with a sense of urgency not seen since last orders were called at the pub where she'd held her doomed engagement party, she tossed her jacket over a chair, uncorked a bottle of red and plucked two steaks from the fridge just as Munro walked through the door.

'I'm glad to see you've got your priorities right,' he said. 'You cook, I'll pour.'

'That sounds fair,' said West, rolling her eyes. 'You're grinning like a halfwit, what's going on?'

'I was simply musing on the benefits of airbags, that's all.'

'What are you talking about?'

'Nothing, Charlie,' said Munro as he handed her a glass. 'Here. Your very good health. Although, there is another reason for my, shall we say, joyous disposition.'

'And what's that then?'

'I've some good news, if you're interested in hearing it.'

'Of course I am! What is it? Have they finished your house?'

'Good grief, you know well enough that'll not be for weeks yet.'

'Well, what then?'

'I've decided to take up volunteering.'

'Excellent!' said West. 'Might stop you moping around the house wondering what to do with your time. So, what is it? Help the Aged?'

'I'll crown you.'

'Alright, some homeless charity, then? I don't know!'

'Police Scotland.'

West, looking completely perplexed, lowered her glass and stared blankly at Munro.

'You've lost me,' she said.

'I had a word with George and he's not averse to the suggestion, in fact, I rather got the impression he's quite keen on it.'

'You mean you can be a volunteer with the force?'

'Oh, aye,' said Munro. 'It's quite common.'

'So, how does that work?'

'Well, it's a civilian role of course, there'll be no salary or perks as such, and no rank to speak of.'

'So, you'll just be plain old Jimbo? Mr Munro?'

'Correct. Once he's gone through the motions and had the request approved, I shall be taking on the role of… well, let's just say advisor, for now.'

'Well, that's great news!' said West. 'I'm made up for you. Really, I am. I always knew you weren't ready to jack it in. So, we've not seen the back of you yet, eh?'

'You have not,' said Munro. 'Not yet. There is one other thing – I shall be answerable to you.'

'What?'

'You're the boss, Charlie. Your wish is my command.'

Slightly unnerved by the imminent role reversal, West eased herself into a chair, thought for moment, and raised her glass.

'I'm not sure about that,' she said.

'How so?'

'Dunno. It just doesn't seem right, somehow. Me telling you what to do. It's not the natural order of things.'

'Utter tosh, Charlie. Besides, you wouldn't dare. No, no, in my official capacity as the man on the street I shall simply be at liberty to offer you the benefit of my experience, that's all.'

'I don't know.'

'Think about it. Apart from the fact that I'll not be paid, and I'll have no rank, things really won't be that different.'

'Sure?'

'Positive, lassie. Absolutely positive.'

'Well, in that case,' said West, mustering a smile as she raised her empty glass. 'Welcome back. I think. Cheers.'

* * *

With his shirt sleeves rolled to the elbow and a butcher's apron tied around his waist, Munro set about clearing the dishes as the sound of the phone drew West from the sofa interrupting any thoughts she'd had of enjoying a snifter in front of the telly.

'Dougal,' she said, eyeing the bottle of Balvenie sitting on the counter, 'after all that running around you've been doing I'd have thought you'd be in bed by now. You must be shattered.'

'I am, miss, but that's why God gave us Red Bull. And Irn-Bru. And chocolate.'

'I think I've got the picture. Where are you? The noise is terrible.'

'It's the rain, miss. It's hammering down.'

'Well, what on earth are you doing outside at this time of night?'

'It's Jardine's car. We've found it.'

'Blinding!' said West as she clicked her fingers at Munro. 'We're on our way.'

'We?' said Munro, exasperated.

'Yes, Jimbo, we. You've only had one glass, you can drive.'

'I'm not a chauffeur, lassie.'

'You are now,' said West as she held the phone aloft. 'Dougal, where exactly are you?'

'Cumnock, miss. The car park on Ayr road by the Keir McTurk brig.'

'Cumnock?' said Munro. 'By jiminy, it sounds like he's been hounding that Macallan woman again.'

'Okay, Dougal, listen,' said West, grabbing her coat, 'you stay put and keep your head down. Jardine can't be far away.'

'But…'

'I don't want him spooked when he comes back, we need to…'

'…but, miss…'

'…bring him in, nice and calm. See if there's any uniform in the area and tell them to keep their eyes peeled.'

'There's no need!' yelled Dougal, straining to be heard.

'What?'

'I've been trying to tell you, there's no need. We've found him.'

'You've just earned yourself a free lunch. Where is he?'

'He's in the car.'

'Police car?'

'His car. He's stone dead.'

Chapter 9

Looking every inch the tomboy in her dark jeans, black boots and matching baseball cap, West – indistinguishable from her male colleagues – darted across the car park to the shelter of the marquee billowing above the blue BMW coupe, and nudged her way past the SOCOs as Munro, shielding his eyes from the glare of the floodlights, ambled along behind her.

Unperturbed by the sight of the body slumped behind the wheel, she snapped on a pair of gloves and leaned in, intrigued by the puffy eyes, the trickle of blood running from the nose, and the tiny beads of perspiration peppering the forehead when the appearance of a familiar face at the opposite window caused her to jump.

'Christ! You gave me a fright,' she said. 'How come you're here so soon?'

With his towering frame, bushy beard, and honey-brown eyes, Andy McLeod had more in common with an axe-wielding lumberjack than a forensic pathologist.

'Your DS called me,' he said. 'I hear congratulations are in order.'

'Come again?'

'DI?'

'Oh, that,' said West. 'Same job, different title. Is it me, or is there a funny smell round here?'

'It's not you, Inspector. It's this fella. Bowels.'

'Nice. So, how come Dougal called you out so soon?'

'Because he realised our friend here has a raging temperature. Or should I say, had, a raging temperature.'

'Doesn't miss a trick, our Dougal. So, that explains the sweat?'

'Aye, and it's not exactly tropical, is it?'

'Maybe he went for a jog.'

'Well, he's certainly dressed for it,' said McLeod sarcastically.

'First impressions?'

'The possibilities are endless. It could be something viral. Or a cardiac arrest. Or it could be something he's ingested. Either way, I'd like to get him on the slab as soon as possible.'

'Give me ten minutes and he's all yours,' said West. 'When do you think you might…'

'I'll call you tomorrow. I should have something by then.'

'Nice one. Oh, time of death. I don't suppose you…'

'Indeed I do. His temperature's still above normal, so some time within the last hour I'd say – ninety minutes, tops.'

West, looking startled, stared at McLeod, held his gaze for a moment and turned to Munro.

'Dougal?' she said. 'Is he…?'

'In the car, lassie. Drying off.'

Munro, impressed with West's sudden surge of enthusiasm – an emotion normally reserved for breakfast, lunch, and dinner – nodded politely at McLeod and turned his attention to the cadaver as West sprinted back to the Peugeot.

'Dougal!' she said as she yanked open the door. 'Look, I know it's late, and I know you're knackered, but I need your help, big time.'

'No bother, miss. Name it.'

'Cameras.'

'None here,' said Dougal, 'I've already checked.'

'Crap. He's only been dead an hour, we need to find out where the nearest cameras are and we need to know if anyone was with him, or at least which direction he came from, can you do that?'

'I'll do my best, just give me a minute.'

* * *

A sullen-faced West, hands in pockets, sidled up to Munro, her cheeks puffing as she heaved a sigh.

'What's up with you, Charlie?'

'I'll tell you what's up. When I was in London there were cameras everywhere; on every corner, at every junction, you couldn't get away from them. I hated it. It was like living with Big Brother.'

'And now?'

'I miss them. I flipping well miss them like mad.'

* * *

Dougal, still wearing his crash helmet in an effort to stave off the rain, called out to West as he rushed towards her.

'Miss,' he said, catching his breath, 'the only camera nearby is outside the community hospital down the road, if there's nothing on that then we'll have to go miles in each direction to reach the next.'

'Oh, that's just great,' said West, 'it's like living in the bleeding dark ages up here. You may as well give it a go, Dougal, you never know, we might get lucky.'

'Miss.'

'Anything we should know about?'

'Not much,' said Dougal. 'If this was a pay and display, we'd know what time he got here from the time on the ticket but...'

'But it's free?'

'Aye.'

'And no-one saw him pull in or…?'

'At this time of night, miss? Out here?'

'Yeah, you're right,' said West. 'I suppose we should count our blessings that we found him at all. Who did find him?'

'The fella in the Astra, over there. We had to move him, he was parked right alongside.'

'And what time was this?'

'About fifteen, maybe twenty minutes before I called you.'

'And he didn't see anyone with Jardine?'

'No, miss,' said Dougal. 'He says he parked here this morning, came back across the pedestrian bridge and called us straight away. Jardine was that close he couldn't open the door.'

'Statement?'

'Done.'

'How is he?'

'A wee bit shaken but aye, I think he's alright.'

'Okay,' said West, 'well, there's no point keeping the poor sod out here, you may as well send him home, and you do the same. Get your head down for a few hours and if I see you before nine o'clock, you're in trouble.'

'Right you are,' said Dougal as he donned his gloves. 'What about the car? There's only so much this lot can do out here in this weather.'

West, momentarily stumped, glanced at Munro for inspiration.

'Tell them to take it in as soon as we're done,' he said. 'Strip it down, see if he's got anything stashed away, and tell them to dust every nook and cranny. A set of prints other than Jardine's may be the only chance we have of finding out what really happened here.'

* * *

Crouching by the passenger side door, Munro – his nose twitching at the unsavoury smell – waved his flashlight under the seat like an usherette in a theatre and grimaced with disdain.

'Dear God,' he said, 'there's enough rubbish down here to keep a valeting company busy for a day or two.'

'What have you got?' said West.

'Nitrous oxide canisters and a couple of balloons…'

'So, he liked his hippy crack, then.'

'Aye. And some empty crisp packets, a glove, a parking ticket, a rotten banana, and no doubt a selection of local wildlife. How about you?'

West reached inside his jacket and retrieved a wallet and a folded white envelope.

'There's a wad of cash in here,' she said, 'the keys are in the ignition, and his phone's in his lap.'

'Call log?' said Munro as he turned his attention to the glove compartment, rifling through the contents with the tip of a biro.

'Just a tick,' said West, 'as long as we don't need a password, then we should be able to get in. Right, he's called the same number a hundred times, all within the last couple of hours, but the log's showing each call only lasted a second or two.'

'Which means?'

'Which means,' said West, 'he dialled and hung up. It was probably engaged and he didn't want to leave a message.'

'I don't suppose it was nine, nine, nine, was it?'

'Should have been, if he'd had any sense. Nope, it's someone called "Fou". Maybe his girlfriend's foreign.'

'Spell it.'

'F-O-U.'

'It's a French word, Charlie,' said Munro as he stood, desperate for a breath of fresh air. 'It means crazy, mad, like radge or nutter.'

'Well, that's not a name then, is it?' said West. 'Unless… unless it's a kind of nickname.'

'Aye, could be.'

'Hold up, French, you say? The bank he worked for is French.'

'Then,' said Munro, 'I dare say that that's where this Fou fellow works as well.'

'I'll get one of the boys to trace it tomorrow.'

'Anything else?'

West lifted the cuff on Jardine's left arm.

'Breitling,' she said, 'that must've cost a bob or two, and on the other – the same as Byrne – he had a string of beads wrapped around his wrist, too.'

'Is that what trendy young bankers are wearing these days?'

'Must be,' said West, frowning as she caught a faint whiff of sandalwood. 'But what I don't get is, why Mala beads?'

'You'll have to explain, Charlie.'

West stood, walked around the car and perched on the bonnet.

'It's a Buddhist thing, Jimbo,' she said, folding her arms. 'Each string has a hundred and eight beads which represents the number of Kleshas.'

'And Kleshas are?'

'Negative stuff, stuff that clouds the mind like anxiety, depression, anger, that kind of thing. You use the beads to keep your mind focused while you're counting off mantras when you're meditating, or chanting, or something.'

'So, they're like rosary beads?'

'Yeah, if you like.'

'I'm impressed, Charlie,' said Munro as he turned for the car, 'and where did you achieve such a state of educational enlightenment?'

'The Holy Isle,' said West. 'Well, I had to do something to take my mind off the lentil soup, didn't I?'

* * *

Munro started the engine, turned the heater up full blast, and sat staring pensively through the windscreen as Jardine's body was loaded into the back of the ambulance.

'Those beads,' he said, 'you're absolutely certain they're Mala beads and not just any old…'

'Positive,' said West. 'Why?'

'Well, if what we're led to believe is true, Charlie, I simply cannae see Byrne or Jardine being into that kind of thing.'

'Well, they're certainly not the type to go for a night of spiritual cleansing over a pint in the pub, granted, but I think your mind's working overtime, Jimbo. I doubt they even knew what they are, they probably picked them up in some trendy boutique as a fashion accessory.'

'Aye, maybe you're right,' said Munro as they left the car park. 'Maybe you're right.'

Chapter 10

As a naïve, young rookie Duncan Reid had hoped his inaugural case as a DC would be a gritty, hair-raising adventure crawling through the underbelly of the criminal world grappling with gangsters and maniacal murderers in a bid to rid the streets of undesirables.

Instead, he was left sorely disappointed when, as the junior investigating officer, he was assigned the more menial tasks to tackle while the rest of the team attempted to solve the riddle of the body on the beach.

However, with a drug-related death on his hands, a missing batch of Buprenorphine, and a dead goat to deal with, he grasped the opportunity to prove his mettle by embracing his role with renewed vigour.

With a match dangling from his lips and his face illuminated by the glow of the screen, he sat studying the footage from the Crisis Centre as a weary West, looking much the worse for wear, bumbled through the door and switched on the lights.

'Good party, was it?' he said, grinning.

'Let's just say the host was dead on his feet. Coffee please, make it a strong one, and something edible, if there's anything there.'

'Still some ginger nuts left,' said Duncan. 'Unlike you to be out on a school night, miss. It must've been some gig.'

'It was,' said West. 'If you like The Grateful Dead. It's Jardine. We found his car.'

'Result!'

'And he was in it.'

'Even better.'

'He was dead.'

'Oh. Well, I've got something to cheer you up. Take a look at this.'

'First things first,' said West as she threw her jacket to one side, slumped in a seat and put her feet on the desk. 'I've got a job for you.'

Duncan flung his head back and sighed despondently.

'It's not more filing or running for sandwiches, is it?' he said, handing her a mug.

'Nope. I need you to take a look around Jardine's flat. Get on to Glasgow and tell them you need the big key to get in. And if you get any hoo-ha from them, tell them to give me a call.'

'Roger that, miss. And thanks.'

'For what?'

'I just thought you'd rather send Dougal, that's all.'

'Nah, he deserves a break.'

'Where is he, anyway? It's not like him to be late.'

'He's never late, Duncan. He's always early. Besides, he's having a lie-in.'

Much to West's chagrin, Dougal – looking as bright as a button with his neatly-parted hair and immaculately-pressed chinos – appeared in the doorway clutching a paper carrier bag.

'Then again,' she said. 'Maybe he isn't.'

'Alright!' said Dougal as he placed the bag in front of her. 'I thought you might be hungry. There's two fried egg, two square sausage, and two bacon.'

'Dougal, I could kiss you.'

'Not necessary, miss. Really, not necessary.'

'And Duncan,' said West as she helped herself to a toastie, 'I don't want a repeat of last time, take a proper look round, bring back anything relevant, and anything you can't shift, take a photo. Got it?'

'Where are you off to?' said Dougal.

'Jardine's flat.'

'Rather you than me, it's still plopping down out there.'

'I'm glad you feel like that, Dougal,' said West as she dusted the crumbs from her fingers before diving in for a second helping, 'because I need you here. Jardine's financial records. We need to get a handle on this loan racket he's been operating. I want everything you can get your hands on: payslips, current account, savings, you know the score. Let's see what he's been up to.'

'Miss.'

'Oh, and here's his phone. The last person he called was a geezer called Fou.'

'Fou?'

'Some kind of nutter, if Jimbo's French is anything to go by. Get a trace on the number, will you? Find out who he is and where he lives. Right, Duncan, what have you got?'

Duncan grabbed his laptop, set it down in front of West and stood back as she and Dougal, looking over her shoulder, watched a furtive Mary Ferguson, captured by a ceiling-mounted camera, help herself to the Buprenorphine from an unlocked cupboard with the speed and agility of a pickpocket on London's Oxford Street while her counsellor chatted with a caller at the door.

'Bloody hell!' said West, astonished at the accuracy of her supposition. 'I was right after all.'

'Aye, you were,' said Duncan. 'Well, half right, miss. All we have to do now is prove that she's the one who gave it to Byrne.'

'Is she still at the hospital? I can't see her going back to Glasgow without talking to Craig.'

'Give me a second and I'll find out.'

'There is nothing more welcoming,' said Munro as he entered the office, shaking the rain from his cap, 'than the smell of freshly baked bread, or indeed bacon, for that matter.'

'Where have you been?' said West. 'I thought you were right behind me?'

'I was, lassie, the difference is, I wasnae travelling at eighty miles an hour.'

'You'll never travel at eighty miles an hour,' said West, 'not in that clapped out thing of yours. Come on, breakfast, get it before it goes cold.'

Munro hung his coat on a hanger and, averting his eyes, placed his hand in the carrier bag as if fumbling for a raffle ticket in a lucky dip.

'Square sausage!' he said, content with his prize. 'Thanking you.'

'So,' said West, 'what's the plan, Mr Munro?'

'Mr Munro?' said Dougal. 'Not Jimbo? What's going on?'

'I'm away to see George,' said Munro, 'and all being well, when I return, you will have the undeniable pleasure of working with a retired detective and a civilian volunteer willing to impart the benefit of his experience, should you need it.'

'Does that mean you're coming back?'

'Aye, laddie. I'm coming back. Now, if you'll excuse me.'

'Miss,' said Duncan as Munro straightened his tie and left the room, 'Mary Ferguson; she's staying at the Abbotsford Hotel, Corsehill Road. It's a ten-minute drive from the hospital, if that.'

Duncan turned the collar up on his beaten, leather jacket and replaced the match in his mouth as West finished her coffee, grabbed her coat, and left the room.

'Dougal,' he said, with a wry grin, 'Westy's birthday, is that anytime soon?'

'Search me,' said Dougal. 'Why?'

'I was going to get her a copy of *Leadership for Dummies*, but I don't think I'll bother.'

* * *

Having had his fair share of thrills and spills as a daunting uniformed presence on the streets of Ayrshire, DCI Elliot enjoyed a largely sedentary lifestyle, free from the uncertainty of what lay around the corner and the heart-stopping shock of sudden surprises. Or so he thought.

'For the love of God, James! What the hell are you doing here!'

Munro, hidden by the shadows of the darkened office, crossed his legs and smiled as he reclined in the comfort of an armchair.

'Morning, George,' he said. 'How are you?'

'How am I? How do you think? I wasn't expecting to see you here so early! For goodness sake, this is my office!'

'You're quite right,' said Munro, 'it is indeed. Although I think you'll find your watch may have stopped. It's not early anymore. It's past eight.'

'Eight!' said Elliot, raising his voice. 'Eight! That is early. Where I come from, eight o'clock is… oh, what's the use! What are you after, anyway?'

'I was simply wondering if you'd made any progress with the volunteer position we discussed.'

'It's the morning, James! I've just arrived! What makes you think I've made any progress?'

'Och, it's a terrible trait called optimism,' said Munro. 'It tends to afflict the more gullible members of society.'

'Does it, indeed?' said Elliot, as one corner of his mouth lifted in a half smile. 'Does it indeed. I had Beef Wellington for my supper last night. Did I tell you that?'

'Aye, you did.'

'It had a profound effect on the altruistic side of my nature...'

'Is that so?'

'...compelling me to pursue your request in the comfort of my own home...'

'Most commendable.'

'...much to the annoyance of Mrs Elliot, who described me as no better than a boarder in lodgings.'

'I'm sure she'll get over it,' said Munro. 'So, what's the story?'

'According to the rule book, volunteers are welcomed with open arms but may only be employed after the positions have been advertised and all suitable candidates interviewed.'

'Red tape.'

'Blame the EU. I do.'

'So, tell me,' said Munro, 'what positions do you have available?'

Elliot, becoming flustered, twitched nervously in his seat in much the same way a Doberman might when intimidated by a Chihuahua.

'The youth volunteer scheme,' he said, deliberately muffling his words. 'We need adult volunteers to work with a handful of kids, to get their point of view, so we can work towards building a brighter...'

Elliot's words tailed off as a stony-faced Munro stared right through him.

'Never work with weans or animals,' he said. 'You know that.'

'Quite right, James, quite right. Well, how about this: custody visitor?'

'You're actually suggesting I visit villains in their cells to ask how they're being treated?'

'You'll not be alone. The visits are made in pairs.'

'Is that it?'

'I'm afraid so, James.'

'Well, that's me away, then.'

'Where to?'

'I hear Beachy Head's quite nice at this time of year.'

'Sit down, man! I'm joking you!'

'You know me, George. I dinnae have a sense of humour.'

'No,' said Elliot. 'I forgot. Front desk. Twelve midnight to six am. Three days a week.'

'Och, I've had enough of this,' said Munro. 'This conversation is over.'

'Take it, James.'

'You must be out of your mind.'

'See here, it's an old post that's never been filled. We don't actually need anyone anymore.'

Munro hovered by the door and cocked his head to one side.

'I get the distinct feeling there's some chicanery involved here, George.'

'That all depends on how you look at it,' said Elliot. 'Listen, James, the post is still open, you fill it, job done and no-one's the wiser. And if you enjoy your role and wish to work five days a week, then I'll not stop you. And of course, you'd be at liberty to wander around the building and mingle with your old colleagues. Do you understand what I'm saying?'

'I never had you down as rule bender, George. Are you not putting your neck on the line?'

'Let me worry about that. The fact of the matter is, we need the help and you can provide it. It's up to you.'

Munro opened the door and turned to face Elliot as he pondered the offer.

'Just to be clear,' he said, 'You're not expecting me to be here in the wee hours, are you?'

'Of course not.'

'In that case, I accept. Thanking you, George. Thanking you.'

* * *

As a fine example of Scottish Baronial architecture, the ivy-clad Abbotsford Hotel, once surrounded by rolling, green fields rather than an abundance of tarmac was, nonetheless, a welcoming sight when compared to the type of budget accommodation West had been expecting.

Taken aback by the vaulted ceiling, open fires, and a profusion of period panelling, West – likening it to a stately home normally overrun by coachloads of fee-paying visitors – wiped her feet and, feeling somewhat underdressed, approached the front desk.

'Morning,' she said as the rain dripped from her cuffs. 'I've come to see one of your guests: Mary Ferguson.'

The young gent on reception, smartly attired in a crisp, white shirt, raised his eyebrows and smiled knowingly.

'Oh, aye,' he said softly, his manner akin to that of an undertaker greeting a widow at his funeral parlour. 'She checked in last night with a wee bairn and, I might add, no luggage.'

'Her husband's in the hospital,' said West defensively. 'It was an emergency.'

'Sorry. I never realised. Who shall I say is asking for her?'

'DI West.'

The receptionist, his cheeks flushing with embarrassment, turned his back as he dialled the room, his voice a barely audible whisper.

'She says you're to go straight up. Top of the stairs, it's right opposite. I'll send some tea. On the house.'

* * *

Half expecting to meet Rhett Butler as she made her way up the sweeping staircase, West reached the first floor just as Mary Ferguson, wrapped in a towelling robe and looking as though she hadn't slept in weeks, opened the door.

'That's a relief,' she said. 'I wasn't expecting a woman.'

'Is it alright if I come in?' said West. 'I wouldn't want to wake the baby. I can wait downstairs if you'd like.'

'No, you're alright,' said Mary, 'he's away with the fairies just now, dreaming like a good 'un.'

West took a seat by the dressing table as Mary checked the cot before easing herself onto the bed.

'Well, you've not come to give me bad news,' she said, 'the hospital will do that. So, how can I help?

'It's just a few questions. I know you've already spoken to DC Reid but…'

'No bother. I was probably off with the fella, anyway. He didn't exactly catch me at a good time.'

'No,' said West. 'I'm sure. Look, I won't waste your time going over old ground, obviously you've no idea who attacked your husband?'

'No, I have not.'

'It's more to do with money.'

'How so?'

'Craig's been unemployed for a while now, right?'

'Aye, that's right.'

'So, I need to know how you get by. I understand he gives you an amount each month, what you might call living expenses. Any idea where it comes from, if he's not earning?'

'No,' said Mary. 'I've never questioned it. He used to earn a packet so I've just assumed he's had it sitting in his account.'

'Okay, and neither of you claim any benefits? Jobseekers? Child benefit? That kind of thing?'

'No. Never have. Never will.'

West, leaning forward with her elbows on her thighs, rubbed her chin and looked up at Mary.

'Your brother's pretty well-off, isn't he?' she said. 'Sean?'

'Aye. Minted. Not that I'll ever see any of it.'

'You don't get on?'

'Chalk and cheese,' said Mary. 'Besides, he's not exactly generous. It's like they say, the more you've got, the tighter you become.'

'Is there anyone else in your family? Brothers? Sisters?'

'No. Just us.'

'Parents?'

'Both long gone.'

'So, you're his next of kin?'

'Aye, I suppose I am.'

'In that case,' said West, taking a deep breath, 'I'm afraid I've got some bad news for you. He's dead.'

Mary glanced at West, her face breaking into a lacklustre smile.

'Oh, well,' she said, shrugging her shoulders. 'It had to happen sooner or later, I suppose. Probably picked on the wrong fella, is that it?'

'Maybe,' said West. 'We're still looking into it, we only found him last night.'

Mary pulled the robe around her tight and folded her arms.

'Let's hope the bugger didn't make a will.'

'Sorry?'

'If there's no will, and I'm next of kin, then I'll be quids in, right?'

'Yup, I suppose you will,' said West. 'So, you're not upset, then?'

'No. Frankly, it's about time lady luck paid me a visit. God knows I could I use it.'

West, surprised at Mary's lack of emotion, stood up, drove her hands deep into her pockets, and leaned against the door.

'There's something else I need to ask you about,' she said. 'Your treatment. The programme you're on.'

'That DC told you, did he?'

'As you'd expect.'

'Aye. Fair enough. What about it?'

'You're on Buprenorphine,' said West. 'Is that right?'

'Aye.'

'Okay, well, I don't mean to sound blunt, but why'd you nick it?'

Mary stared at West, held her gaze, and moved to the cot, swallowing hard as she cleared her throat.

'We've got you on film,' said West. 'CCTV. It's all over the place.'

'So, what happens now?' said Ferguson. 'You do me for theft and I lose the bairn?'

'No. It doesn't have to work like that. I just need to know why.'

Mary returned to the bed and sat with her head bowed, hands clasped tightly in her lap.

'The money from Craig,' she said. 'It didn't come this month.'

'He stopped the transfers?'

'There were no transfers. It was always cash.'

'And?'

'He said he'd had problems, that there was nothing to worry about and he'd sort it. I'd just have to wait, that's all.'

'So, what did you do?'

'What do you think?' said Mary. 'I took the 'prenorphine. Ten quid a tab. There's a couple of desperate junkies who'll give me twenty.'

'So, you sold it?'

'Aye, what else was I going to do with it? I'm not about to up my own prescription now, am I? Getting hooked on opioids, that's just as bad as…'

'Okay, point taken. So, was this the first time?'

'No. I took some before. But just the once, mind. Straight up.'

'I believe you,' said West as she slowly paced the room. 'Tell me, what do you know about a bloke by the name of Alan Byrne?'

'Byrne? Sean's pal?'

'That's him.'

'Nutter.'

'Do you know he died recently?'

'Are you joking me? When?'

'Like I said. Recently.'

'And you think there's a connection between him and Sean?'

'Nah, doubt it,' said West, 'but it's something we have to look at.'

'Well, forgive me if I don't sound too charitable, but they both deserve it. Nasty pieces of work, the pair of them.'

'I don't suppose Byrne was one of the people you flogged the 'prenorphine to, was it?'

'Are you joking?' said Mary, sheepishly. 'What makes you think I sold it to Byrne?'

'Because he died of an overdose. A Buprenorphine overdose.'

'Oh,' said Mary as her face blanched, 'now I see where this is going. You think I did it? You think I killed him?'

'Actually, I don't think you did,' said West, keeping her cards close to her chest. 'I don't think you're that stupid.'

Mary, looking decidedly uneasy, flinched as the knock on the door interrupted their conversation.

'Come in,' she said nervously.

West's eyes lit up as the young man from reception backed into the room carrying a large tray laden with a teapot, two cups, a rack of toast, a selection of jams and marmalades, and two buttered scones.

'Mrs Ferguson,' he said, fearful of waking the baby, 'we were sorry to hear about your husband and thought a wee something might cheer you up.'

'That's very kind of you,' said West as he left the room. 'I must be going too, thanks for your time.'

'Aye, okay,' said Mary. 'You're welcome.'

'Are you staying here or heading back to Glasgow?'

'Here. Until he wakes up. And then some, I imagine.'

'Good,' said West as she filched a slice of toast. 'We might need another chat.'

* * *

Unimpressed with the plethora of pretentious brasseries, ritzy restaurants, designer boutiques, and delicatessens touting artisan loaves for the price of a Sunday roast with all the trimmings, Duncan – who shopped for clothes in the department store, lived off takeaways, and preferred the atmosphere of his down-at-heel local to the over-priced bars of Merchant City – parked behind the patrol car on Miller Street and wandered over.

'Alright, pal?' he said, flashing his warrant card as the uniformed officer lowered the window. 'Are you two here for me?'

The officer in passenger seat leaned forward to get a glimpse of the scruffy detective.

'Aye,' he said. 'We hear you forgot your key.'

'That's good, that. So, what does that make you? A locksmith?'

The driver opened his door and scurried round to the boot.

'As it happens,' he said, grinning as he retrieved the battering ram, 'it does! I love using this, pure magic. So, how come you're up this neck of the woods? Is this not something we should be dealing with?'

'I wish it was,' said Duncan, 'but see, the fella who lives here, he was topped on our patch so it's up to us to clear up the mess.'

'Fair enough. Let's hope the neighbours are out, I'd hate to wake them. So, where are we?'

'Top floor. Number one.'

* * *

As someone who'd grown up on a housing scheme in the arse end of Inverclyde, the notion of squandering half a million pounds on a city apartment just because of the location was folly enough, but to skimp on the ironmongery, was pure madness.

Standing well clear, Duncan allowed himself a wry smile as the solid hardwood door all but flew off its hinges with a single whack from the big red key prompting the lead officer to beckon him inside while his colleague made arrangements to have the door boarded up.

Snapping on a pair of gloves, he made a cursory tour of the neat but characterless flat, sneering at the laminate flooring and flat-pack furniture, before perching on the sofa and lifting the lid of the laptop sitting on the coffee table.

Initially disheartened by the blank screen, he tapped the space bar with his index finger, his triumphant smile dissipating as it sprang to life only to reveal the browser, still open, plastered with images even a rough-around-the-edges, street-wise cop like Duncan found disturbing. Disgusted by the fact that Jardine's viewing habits appeared to centre around hostage-taking videos and adult websites that featured content of a sado-masochistic nature, he drew a breath and slammed it shut before heading to the bedroom where, in his experience, anyone with something to hide, would hide it.

Compared to the rest of the flat, which resembled a show home for fans of minimalism, the bedroom was in a state of positive disarray; piles of dirty laundry littered the floor, a silk dressing gown in a questionable green and gold Paisley pattern lay strewn across the bed, and a jar of Anadrol – a substance he recognised as the steroid of choice amongst the bodybuilding fraternity – sat beside a tumbler of water on the bedside table.

Sliding open the left-hand side of the mirrored, double wardrobe, Duncan – not one for dressing to the nines – stared in amazement at the number of suits crammed onto the rail alongside a collection of blue, white-collared shirts and questioned why anyone with an eye for sartorial elegance would have the need for combat fatigues, a black, woollen balaclava, or indeed, a pair of commando boots.

Optimistically anticipating the haul of the century, he tentatively slid open the other side of the wardrobe and whistled in disbelief at the kind of cache Rambo would be proud of.

Standing back, he pulled the phone from his pocket and reeled off half a dozen photos before tapping in an inventory of Jardine's stash: two Remington .22 air rifles, three air pistols – one Ruger, one Webley, and one Heckler and Koch – three tins of pellets, a tub of steel ball bearings, a twelve-inch Bowie knife, and, the icing on the cake, a Redback tactical crossbow which, disconcertingly, looked capable of inflicting more damage than the rest of his arsenal put together.

'Alright pal?' said the officer with the battering ram as he appeared in the doorway. 'Anything I can help you with?'

'Aye,' said Duncan, grinning. 'I need to bag this lot, then that's me away.'

Chapter 11

Although West, on occasion, had done her best to convince him that his boyish good looks would pay dividends later in life when he'd look considerably younger than his greying contemporaries, and the dire state of his love life was simply down to bad luck, Dougal – looking forward to the day when he'd have to shave out of necessity rather than habit – remained unconvinced. He sat at his desk with the same petrified look of inevitability as a deep sea diver who'd run out of air.

'Blimey,' she said, 'what's up with you? You look like you've wet yourself.'

'Not far off, miss,' said Dougal, 'if I'm honest. It's Emily. She's asked me out again.'

'Emily?'

'Aye, you remember, the lassie who worked for Gundersen before we nicked him. The lassie who got hammered on our first date.'

'Oh, her! But I thought you liked her?'

'I did, aye. She's gorgeous. And clever, too.'

'So, what did she say?'

'She was wondering why I'd not been in touch. I didn't have the heart to tell her I couldn't handle her drinking.'

'Och, Dutch courage, laddie,' said Munro. 'We've all been there.'

'Maybe, boss, but she was out cold by seven-thirty. Two bottles of wine to herself.'

'Sounds like a lightweight,' said West, smirking.

'Listen to me,' said Munro, 'remember as a wean, if there was a lassie in the playground who caught your eye, would you tell her so?'

'Don't be daft.'

'Exactly. Instead, you'd call her names and tease her, too scared to show your true colours. This is no different. She simply had a wee drink to calm her nerves...'

'A wee drink?'

'...and got carried away.'

'Jimbo's right,' said West. 'What you've got to remember, Dougal, is that you've seen her at her worst, and she knows that. Now, embarrassed as she must be, if she's got the balls to call you back, then she must like you, too.'

'Aye! I never thought of it like that.'

'And she's not likely to make the same mistake again,' said Munro. 'Take my advice and give her a call, laddie. You'll not regret it.'

'You think so?'

'I know so. Life's too short for "what ifs". Trust me.'

'Anyway,' said West, 'counselling session over, how'd you get on? With Jardine, I mean.'

'Result, miss!' said Dougal, his spirits lifted by the pep talk. 'He's got one of those mobile banking apps on his phone and he's been moving money around like a banker playing the stock market.'

'No surprise there,' said West. 'Do we know where?'

'Aye. Jersey and the Isle of Man, mainly. The fella's loaded.'

'Tax evasion?'

'Spot on. See, he's not on the payroll with the bank, he's registered as self-employed so he's liable for his own tax and last year he paid less than me.'

'Pity,' said West, 'if he hadn't kicked the bucket, we could've done him for that, too. What about this Fou geezer?'

'Claude Foubert. Five-eleven, well-built, no hair and a small birthmark like a port wine stain on his forehead. Age: thirty-seven. Single. Born: Maisons-Laffitte; that's a posh part of Paris. He's been over here with the bank for three and a half years.'

'Any form?'

'Not here, but I've asked the Parisian PP to run a check, see if he's been up to any mischief at home.'

'Nice one. And have you spoken to him?'

'No, no. Not yet,' said Dougal, 'I don't want to scare him off. I think it's best we speak face to face, but that'll mean another trip up to Glasgow. Tea?'

'Yes, please,' said West. 'Do you want to pay him a visit, or shall we send Duncan?'

'I'm not fussed.'

'Well, think about it. Either way, if Foubert's a part of Jardine's gang, then we'll need some evidence to nick him, as well.'

Dougal handed out the mugs and placed the tin of ginger nuts on the desk.

'That's all we have left,' he said. 'How was Mary Ferguson, miss? Any joy?'

'Yup. Pity, really. She's a nice kid.'

'Pity?' said Munro. 'How so?'

'She's guilty as hell.'

'Really? Talk us through it then, Charlie.'

'Okay,' said West, sipping her brew. 'For a start, she's the obvious link between Byrne and Jardine…'

'By default, lassie. It doesnae give her cause to kill Byrne.'

111

'Hear me out. Craig Ferguson loses his job, right? He's skint. He goes to Jardine, gets a loan, can't pay it back. Then he starts getting hassled by Byrne. Mary Ferguson swipes the 'prenorphine and they knock him off to get him off their backs.'

'Did Mary Ferguson mention anything about the loan?'

'No,' said West. 'She claims they've been living off money Craig had saved before he got the boot.'

'Sorry, Charlie,' said Munro, 'but if you dinnae mind me saying so, there appears to be a great deal of supposition on your part.'

'You say supposition, I say instinct,' said West, biting into a biscuit. 'The thing is, Jimbo, when I mentioned Alan Byrne, she went all cagey, she was holding back. She knows more than she was letting on.'

'Miss,' said Dougal, 'do you not think it's a bit extreme, though? I mean, killing Alan Byrne just to get out of debt?'

'You think so? Look at the reputation they've got. If you ask me, it was a case of them or us. With Byrne out of the way, they're off the hook, scot free. Let's face it, she may not see eye to eye with her brother but he's hardly going to come after her knowing she's penniless with a baby.'

'Fair enough,' said Dougal.

'And what about the loose ends, Charlie?' said Munro. 'Craig Ferguson and Rona Macallan?'

'Easy,' said West. 'Jardine hears about Byrne's death, puts two and two together, and gives Craig a bloody good hiding to teach him a lesson but he still wants his money back. Now, I know this bit's a bit foggy but, assuming Jardine knew that his brother-in-law was having an affair with Rona Macallan, and he hasn't got a cat's chance in hell of getting his money back from him, who would he go after?'

'Rona Macallan,' said Dougal.

'In one,' said West. 'Ladies and gentlemen of the jury, I rest my case. And that's why I want to bring her in. You're not saying much, Jimbo, what do you think?'

Munro drained his cup and wandered to the window where he stood, hands clasped behind his back, watching the clouds roll by.

'What do I think of your intentions, Charlie?' he said. 'Or what do I think, as in, my opinion?'

'Your opinion.'

'Well,' said Munro, 'as Dougal says, your theory's plausible, I'll give you that, but there's too many gaps for my liking and not enough hard evidence to prove that she was behind Byrne's murder. Add to that the fact that Byrne and Jardine, close friends no less, both died within days of each other, then there's every chance that there's a link between their deaths. If I were dealing with this case, Charlie, I'd hold off for the results of the post-mortem on Jardine before going any further.'

'Okay,' said West, 'but to be honest, if you'd been with me when I questioned Mary Ferguson, then…'

'If it transpires that Jardine died of natural causes, then you might be in with a chance. But if there's anything to suggest otherwise…'

'Well, I'm going to take a flyer on it,' said West indignantly, 'and if I'm wrong, we let her go. What have we got to lose?'

Munro, unrattled by the kerfuffle outside, watched the reflection in the window as Duncan barged through the door weighed down with several clear plastic bags bound with cable ties.

'And there was I thinking you'd be glad to see me,' he said as he stared at their glum faces. 'Any chance of a brew?'

'I'll do it,' said West as she reached for the kettle. 'We're just having a difference of opinion, that's all.'

'I hope that's all it is,' said Duncan. 'Chief. This is for you.'

Munro turned and smiled as he caught sight of the pistol bow.

'Jeez-oh!' said Dougal, 'that looks terrifying.'

'It is,' said Munro, 'in the wrong hands. It's all yours, laddie.'

Dougal grabbed a pair of scissors from his desk drawer, cut open the top of the bag and, taking care not to handle the bow, carefully ran his middle finger along the barrel, wincing as it ran over a burr.

'Exhibit A,' he said, smiling, 'in our first ever case of capricide.'

'Well, that's one loose end tied up,' said Munro. 'I'll drive over to Macallan's tomorrow and let her know.'

'You should tell her about Jardine, too,' said West. 'It'll stop her worrying every time there's a knock at the door.'

'I'll do that, Charlie. Duncan, that's a veritable armoury you have there. Does that all belong to Jardine?'

'Certainly does, chief. And there's more.'

Duncan heaved a large, canvas holdall from his shoulder, retrieved a collection of small bags, and placed them in a neat row on the desk.

'Ammo,' he said, 'various kinds including bolts for the crossbow. Plus some cash, I'm guessing there's about five grand there. Laptop...'

'I'll take that,' said Dougal, 'I can't wait to see what's on it.'

'I'd do it on an empty stomach if I were you, pal, the stuff on there is X-rated. It's not for the faint-hearted, trust me. Oh, and I've got these, too. Steroids.'

'Steroids?' said West as she examined the plastic bottle. 'You mean, like the stuff athletes take?'

'Not athletes, miss,' said Duncan. 'Cheats. And numptys like Jardine. This stuff doesn't just bulk you out, it fries your brain too.'

'Well, that just adds weight to my argument,' said West, 'in so much as he's got the right kind of temperament to knock seven shades out of someone and not give a toss about it. In fact, if Mary Ferguson felt threatened, then there might even be a case for self-defence. We should bring her in. Sorry, Jimbo.'

'It's your call, lassie. You must do what you think is right.'

* * *

West, torn between siding with Munro's suggestion to wait, and stamping her authority on the investigation, found herself caught in a crisis of confidence as she pulled her phone from her hip.

'Saved by the bell,' she said, muttering under her breath. 'It's McLeod.'

She put the phone on speaker, turned up the volume, and placed it in the centre of her desk.

'Andy,' she said. 'How's it going?'

'Very well, Inspector,' said McLeod. 'Very well, indeed. Is this a good time to talk about this Jardine fella?'

'Couldn't be better. We're all here, so fire away.'

'Okay, you can expect a full report just as soon as I find time to type it up, meanwhile, this might give you cause to raise a glass or two.'

'I hope so,' said West. 'God knows I could do with a lift.'

'First off,' said McLeod, 'we found high levels of oxymetholone in his system…'

'Anadrol,' said Duncan.

'Exactly. He must have been on it for years. His heart's abnormally stressed and his liver's on the way out. If he hadn't ended up on my slab, he'd have been up for a transplant within a couple of years.'

'So, that's what killed him?' said West, crossing her fingers. 'It was a heart attack?'

'No, no,' said McLeod, 'nothing of the sort. It was the fever.'

West, completely flummoxed, glanced around the room, her eyes settling on Munro.

'Fever?' she said. 'Well, that's bonkers. Are you telling me he got bitten by a mosquito, or had flu, or something?'

McLeod laughed.

'No.'

'It's not funny, I'm being serious. How the hell can you die from a fever?'

'With the greatest of ease, Inspector. If you have a fever, it must be kept under control. If the body temperature reaches one hundred and eight degrees, then it's goodnight Vienna. That is the critical point when all the internal organs begin to shut down. It's commonly known as multiple organ failure.'

'Bloody hell,' said West, slumping in her chair. 'So, that's why he was sweating his pants off?'

'Exactly,' said McLeod.

'Okay, I know I'm going to regret asking this but if he didn't have flu, then what brought it on?'

'Buprenorphine.'

'Crap.'

'Not the answer you were looking for?'

'I'm not sure. I'm really not sure anymore.'

'The thing is,' said McLeod, 'it wasn't what I'd call a fatal dose, but given the state of his heart and liver, it was enough to polish him off. Incidentally, his condition reminded me of the other fella that came in recently…'

'Alan Byrne?'

'That's him. Cause of death was the same. Far be it for me to tell you how to do your job, but if I were in your shoes, I'd be looking for a link between the two.'

'You don't say,' said West with a sigh. 'As it happens, we do have someone in our sights.'

'I'm glad to hear it. A dealer, I suppose?'

'Nah. Just someone who swiped a load of 'prenorphine from the clinic they attend but who also, coincidentally, had good reason to knock them off.'

'And you think they administered the Buprenorphine?'

'Without a doubt,' said West. 'I mean, probably. They claim they sold it for ten quid a tab but...'

'Let me stop you, there,' said McLeod. 'Tab?'

'Yeah, why?'

'I hate to disappoint you but that's not your man.'

'Come again?'

'If either of these two fellas had taken tablets then I can guarantee we'd have found traces in the stomach, the oesophagus, the duodenum, even the intestines, but there was nothing. The 'prenorphine was taken intravenously.'

'You mean, with a needle?'

'That is the general interpretation of the phrase, aye.'

As the room fell silent, a crestfallen West wandered to the window and stared out across the night sky.

'I've got another phrase for you,' she said curtly. 'Crash and burn.'

'I beg your pardon?'

'Nothing. Look, thanks Andy, I appreciate the call.'

'No bother,' said McLeod. 'One thing before I go, I doubt it has any bearing on the case but your man, Jardine; he was HIV positive.'

Chapter 12

In a rare show of abstinence, West – having said hardly anything all evening – pushed her plate to one side and cradled a glass of red as Munro, fearing she'd succumbed to something terminal, peered over the laptop and sighed as he eyed the half a sirloin lying on the dish.

'For heaven's sake, Charlie,' he said, 'is there something you need to get off your chest? You've had a face like a wet weekend for long enough.'

'Sorry, I'm just…'

'Just what? Feeling sorry for yourself?'

'Something like that.'

'You're better than that, lassie,' said Munro. 'Why?'

'Why do you think? Because I nearly screwed up, that's why.'

'Tosh. You did no such thing. You were following a feasible line of inquiry and had the rug pulled out from under your feet. It happens to the best of us.'

'Thanks,' said West, 'but that doesn't help. I can just see Dougal and Duncan having a good old giggle over this…'

'They'll do no such thing.'

'…they must think I'm a right idiot.'

'You're being too hard on yourself.'

'I just wanted to make a good impression, that's all; first case as a DI and all that.'

'But instead of employing rational thought and using your instinct,' said Munro, 'you let impetuosity get the better of you. You knew in your heart of hearts that Mary Ferguson's no murderer.'

'Yeah, I suppose so,' said West with a sigh, 'I just thought… I thought if I wrapped it up nice and quick, then…'

'Patience,' said Munro, 'is a virtue.'

'You know me, Jimbo, vices are my thing.'

Munro smiled and glanced at the laptop as he sipped his Balvenie.

'Truth be known,' he said, 'if you were that keen to get a conviction, you could have had her for theft, at the very least.'

'I know, but she doesn't deserve that.'

'Well, there's no point moping around here, lassie. You should take yourself to bed and get some rest.'

'Yeah, in a minute,' said West. 'What are you up to on that thing, anyway?'

'Och, just a wee bit of research.'

'Something to do with this volunteer job that you're after?'

'No, no, it's… aye. The volunteer job, that's what it is.'

'So, how'd it go?' said West. 'With Elliot I mean?'

'Done and dusted, Charlie. Officially, I'm on night duty answering the telephone. Unofficially, I am the stone in your shoe.'

'Good. I'm happy for you. When do you start?'

'I already have.'

'Glad to hear it. I don't mind saying, you're a tough act to follow, Jimbo, and having you around will only…'

'Och, stop havering and go to bed. I'm away myself just now. I think I'll read a while before turning in.'

'Okay,' said West. 'I think I'll have a nip of something first then do the same.'

Munro stood, drained his glass, and slipped his spectacles into his breast pocket.

'You're not one for reading, are you, Charlie?'

'If it's the right subject, I am,' said West.

'And what would that be?'

'Menus, mainly.'

'But if you were into reading, what would you fancy? Romance, perhaps?'

'Do me a favour.'

'How about a good murder-mystery then?'

'Busman's holiday.'

'Well, maybe something to keep you up all night?'

'Yeah, that sounds more like it.'

'Good,' said Munro with a smirk. 'I've found just the thing for you. I'll leave it here.'

With no intention of reading anything apart from the label on the second bottle of wine, West watched Munro traipse down the hall before topping up her glass and moving to his chair expecting to be greeted by a Kindle version of "The Exorcist" or "A Nightmare on Elm Street", not a jargon-laden description of Buprenorphine from a pharmaceutical company.

"Vetergesic. Multi-dose solution for Horses and other equidae, dogs and cats. Qualitative Composition: Buprenorphine 0.3mg/ml, as Buprenorphine Hydrochloride 0.324mg/ml, Chlorocresol 1.35mg/ml."

Wishing she'd read the wine label instead, West scoured the website from top to bottom trying to figure out why – in the absence of any pets, and apart from the fact that Vetergesic was just another brand name for Buprenorphine – Munro would think it relevant at all until, scanning the page for a fourth time, her eyes settled on one word: horses.

'You clever bugger,' she said, downing her wine. 'You clever bugger.'

* * *

The unexpected buzz of her phone made her jump.

'Dougal!' she said. 'Do you know what time it is?'

'Aye, sorry miss. Did I wake you?'

'No, it's alright. What's up?'

'Is your email handy?'

'Yeah, hold on.'

'I've got some feedback on Jardine's car,' said Dougal. 'They've found two sets of prints, one belongs to Jardine and the other's unknown. We've no match on the database.'

'Well, that's a big help.'

'I know, but I was thinking they might belong to this Foubert fella, after all, he was the one he called before he keeled over.'

'Good point,' said West. 'We need to have a chat with him. You and Duncan can flip a coin over it, one of you can go up there tomorrow.'

'Right you are, miss. Now, I've also sent you four photos.'

'Okay,' said West. 'Got them.'

'The first three are from Jardine's car; the tyres and the wheel arches. As you'll see, there's a fair bit of muck in there.'

'Yeah, looks like he's been through a field or something.'

'It's a mix of silage, straw and hay.'

'Of course!' said West. 'The road to Macallan's place was plastered with the stuff, so that makes sense.'

'Aye, he probably picked it up when he shot the goat, or afterwards, when he went back to have a pop at her.'

'Well, that's obvious, Dougal. What's your point?'

'My point is, miss, I'd seen it before so I went back and did some checking. Fourth photo; it's the passenger side footwell of Byrne's Range Rover. There's the same mix of straw and hay on the mat.'

'So?'

'So, Byrne's not been near Macallan's place.'

'We don't know that for certain,' said West, 'maybe he went with Jardine to kill the goat.'

'With all due respect, miss, he's hardly likely to come back from the dead just to kill a goat.'

West snorted as she sniggered into her wine glass.

'Sorry, Dougal,' she said, laughing. 'It's late and my mind's all over the shop, so, maybe they went for a reccy beforehand, before Byrne was killed?'

'If they had, there'd be traces of the stuff on the wheels of the Range Rover just like Jardine's Beemer but there isn't. And Byrne didn't get out of his car, the footwell on the driver's side is as clean as whistle.'

'So, what you're saying is…'

'Exactly,' said Dougal. 'Someone apart from Jardine got into Byrne's car.'

* * *

As a firm believer that everything in life was placed on earth to fulfil a preordained role and that anyone or anything attempting to unsettle the status quo could potentially unleash a chain of events with catastrophic consequences for the entire universe, Munro – aware that it was not yet six o'clock – felt a pang of unease as he opened the bedroom door to the smell of burning toast and the sound of spluttering eggs.

'Jumping Jehoshaphat!' he said as he wandered to the kitchen. 'Dinnae tell me you've been at the caffeine again, Charlie.'

'A waste of daylight is a waste of time, Jimbo.'

'Good grief,' said Munro, muttering to himself, 'I'm in the wrong house. I see you've recovered from your bout of self-pity, then.'

'I certainly have,' said West. 'Did you sleep well?'

'I always sleep well, lassie. It's the folk with a guilty conscience that cannae sleep.'

'That explains my insomnia, then. Do you want some breakfast?'

Munro looked on aghast as she dished up a mountain of eggs, bacon, black pudding, sausage, beans and tomatoes, topped off with a tattie scone.

'Well, I can hardly refuse a spread like that,' he said. 'Is that last night's steak on your plate?'

'Yeah. I hate to see it go to waste,' said West. 'It looks like it might stop raining soon.'

'Let's hope so, lassie. It's been dreich for far too long.'

'What are you up to today?'

'I've not thought that far ahead. Why?'

'Fancy a drive?'

'Where to?'

'Out to the country,' said West with a wink. 'I thought we could go see Rona Macallan and tell her we found the goat killer.'

* * *

Despite the glare of the sun bouncing off the rain-soaked asphalt, the road to Tèarmann, Rona Macallan's farmstead – pitted with potholes like plunge pools and littered with fallen branches – posed no problem for the ageing Peugeot as Munro, one hand on the wheel, hurtled along at sixty miles per hour leaving West jostling in her seat like a ragdoll on a rollercoaster ride.

'I'm beginning to see another side of you,' she said, wishing she'd had cereal for breakfast. 'And it's quite dark.'

* * *

Craving a glass of Alka-Seltzer, West, impatient as ever, rattled the letterbox and banged the door filling a startled Macallan with a sense of dread. Arming herself with the trusty poker, she crept downstairs and tentatively opened the door.

'Oh, it's you,' she said, her shoulders slumping with relief. 'With all that banging I thought…'

'I must apologise for my colleague,' said Munro with a reassuring smile, 'she does like to make her presence felt. I do hope we've not interrupted anything.'

Macallan, dressed in a pair of baggy, white sweatpants and a loose-fitting tee shirt, smiled as she tied back her hair and led them through to the kitchen.

'No, you're alright,' she said, 'I was just practising my yoga. Can I get you something?'

'Coffee would be nice,' said West. 'If it's not too much trouble.'

'No trouble at all, Inspector. Mr Munro?'

'Aye. Very kind thanks.'

Struck by the warmth of the antiquated, oil-fired range, Munro slipped off his jacket, took a seat at the dining table, and tipped three heaped teaspoons of sugar into the mug.

'It's only instant,' said Macallan. 'I hope that's okay.'

'That's fine, thanking you,' said Munro, baulking as he took a sip.

'Sorry, I should've said. It's goats' milk.'

'An acquired taste, I think. You'll not mind if I…'

'Not at all, just leave it there. So, have you come to give me some news?'

'We have indeed,' said Munro, smarting from the after-taste. 'I'm glad to report we know who killed Esme.'

'Oh, that's terrific news,' said Macallan. 'At least now I'll have some kind of closure, knowing he's off the streets. Who was it?'

'Sean Jardine.'

'Jardine? The fella who was threatening to do all sorts to me?'

'The same.'

'Do you believe in karma, Miss Macallan?' said West.

'Aye. I do.'

'Good. Because he's dead, too.'

Macallan stared at West with a blank look of bewilderment.

'That is a pity,' she said. 'I wouldn't wish that on anyone. Death, I mean.'

'That's a very generous thing to say, considering what you've been through.'

'Forgiveness frees you from retribution, Inspector.'

'If you say so,' said West, nodding towards her right hand. 'They're nice.'

'Thanks very much,' said Macallan as she toyed with the string of beads wrapped around her wrist. 'They're Malas.'

'I know. Let me guess – Sandalwood.'

'Aye, that's right.'

'Just out of interest, why Sandalwood? I mean why not Citrine? Or Sunstone? Or Sodalite?'

Macallan, both surprised and impressed by West's depth of knowledge on the subject, pulled up a chair and spoke animatedly on the topic.

'It's a personal choice,' she said, 'they all have different qualities. The Citrine, for example, attracts wealth and success and helps to balance the hormones. The Sodalite, that's known as the stone of truth, deepens spiritual perception, but the Sandalwood... the Sandalwood has great healing properties. It can help the immune system recover from almost anything.'

'Almost anything,' said Munro curtly. 'But not everything.'

'How do you mean?'

'Let's just say I have first-hand experience on the matter. How's your pony, Miss Macallan? I forget now, was it Partick or Thistle?'

'If it's the colic you're referring to, Mr Munro, he's fine now, all back to normal.'

'I'm glad to hear it. Tell me, what exactly causes the colic?'

'Oh, more often than not, it comes from eating too much straw, easily done when you're out of haylage. The problem with straw is that it's not easily digested, it compacts in the stomach.'

'And how would you treat it?'

'Well, there's no miracle cure,' said Macallan, 'and if left untreated it can be fatal. No, no, you just have to keep them moving, lunge them a couple of times a day and prevent them from lying down, that only aggravates the condition.'

'I see,' said Munro. 'Fascinating. Truly… fascinating. And that's it?'

'Aye, pretty much. Apart from some pain relief.'

'And that's not a couple of aspirin, is it?' said West.

'Good heavens, no,' said Macallan, laughing gently. 'You need something a wee bit stronger than that, Inspector. An analgesic.'

'Like Vetergesic?'

'Aye! How did you know?'

Macallan craned her neck as she watched West slowly stand, drive her hands into her pockets, and move to the window where she gazed across the field at the goats and the chickens.

'How long have you known Alan Byrne?' she said bluntly.

'Alan Byrne? The name doesn't…'

'He was best mates with Sean Jardine.'

'Oh?'

'Do you not have any of that Sodalite to hand?' said Munro. 'The stone of truth?'

'There's no need to be facetious, Mr Munro.'

'It'll lighten the gravity of the situation, trust me. You see, Miss Macallan, Alan Byrne's dead too.'

Macallan, rankled by the remark, turned to face a scowling West who stood, leaning against the sink with her arms folded, waiting for an answer.

'I'll ask again,' she said. 'How did you meet?'

'Craig.'

'He introduced you?'

'No, no. You see, Craig was having money problems. He told me he'd met this Byrne fella in the pub near work and he'd tapped him for a loan.'

'When was this?'

'When I found out? The weekend before last, I think. Aye, it was the weekend before he was set upon.'

'And were you aware that Craig had lost his job at this point?'

'No,' said Macallan. 'I only found that out when I went to his work a couple of days ago. That's when I met his wife.'

'So, you had no idea he was married, either?'

'No. I did not.'

'He doesn't sound very trustworthy, does he?' said West flippantly. 'What exactly is your relationship with Craig? You obviously get on well together.'

'Aye, we do,' said Macallan. 'We're friends, very good friends.'

'And he likes it here?'

'He does. He can relax here and not worry about trying to prove himself or offending anyone with what he might say. He's vulnerable like that. I think he needs looking after.'

'It sounds to me,' said Munro, 'as though he brings out the maternal side of your nature.'

'More the protective side, Mr Munro.'

'Okay,' said West, 'so back to this loan you were talking about.'

'Oh, aye. Craig said he was getting hassled by this Byrne fella to pay it back.'

'So soon? Did he say how much he owed?'

'No, he never did.'

'So, then what?' said West.

'I was worried for him,' said Macallan, 'he wasn't himself, so when he went back to Glasgow, I gave Byrne a call. I don't have much in the way of savings but I thought if I cleared the debt, that'd get him off his back.'

'How did you get his number?'

'Off Craig's phone, when he wasn't looking.'

'So, you met up with Byrne?'

'I did, aye.'

'Where? Martnaham Loch?'

'The loch? No. It was here. Just the once.'

'He came inside?'

'No, I sat with him in his car,' said Macallan. 'I said I'd pay off the loan and that would be the end of it. I always thought, I don't know why, I always thought it was a couple of hundred but…'

'But it wasn't?'

'No,' said Macallan. 'Byrne said he was into him for fifty grand.'

'Fifty grand?' said West. 'No wonder he didn't worry about paying the mortgage. So, what did you do?'

'What do you think? I told him to forget it. I was raging, with Craig I mean. Then Byrne suddenly went all… creepy.'

'How d'you mean?'

'He said there might be another way of clearing the debt. That he and I could come to some arrangement.'

'So, you told him where to stick it?'

'Right enough. That was the last I saw of him.'

'And did Craig know about this?' said West, reaching for her phone. 'That the two of you had met?'

'No. I was in two minds about telling him, then when he came last weekend he said it was all sorted, that he'd taken care of it. Then when I mentioned what had happened to Esme, that was it. That's when he took off like a shot.'

Macallan glanced at Munro and forced a smile.

'And that's the Sodalite truth,' she said. 'I swear.'

'I appreciate your honesty,' said Munro. 'Would you mind if I used your bathroom before we go?'

'Upstairs. On the left.'

Macallan cleared away the mugs as she waited for West to finish typing a text message before speaking.

'Do you think he'll be okay, Inspector? Craig, I mean?'

'Yeah, I'm sure he will,' said West. 'You should get yourself some Ametrine beads just in case, they're good for optimism.'

* * *

Fumbling in his pockets for a peppermint, a boiled sweet, or even a slither of Kendal Mint Cake, Munro – distracted by an all too common sight – paused to watch a Kestrel hovering against the clear, blue sky before diving at speed towards its unsuspecting prey whilst West, possessed with a similar sense of celerity, raced ahead, jumped in the car, and buckled up.

'You're in an awful hurry, Charlie,' he said as he slipped the keys into the ignition. 'Has the goats' milk had an adverse effect on your physical well-being?'

'No, it tasted fine to me. I got a text from Dougal while you were in the loo, it's Craig Ferguson; he's woken up.'

'Och, you should've said. I'll put my foot down.'

'No, it's alright!' said West, raising her hand. 'There's no rush. Twenty's plenty.'

Pootling along like a short-sighted pensioner on his way to a picnic, Munro carefully weaved his way along the road, cast a sideways glance at West, and smiled softly.

'Did you not want to say something to Miss Macallan before we left, Charlie?'

'No. Like what?'

'Och, I'm not sure, really. Something like: Rona Macallan, I'm arresting you on suspicion of…'

'Yeah, alright,' said West brusquely. 'I'm still thinking about it, okay? I'm still thinking about it.'

'You surprise me, lassie. Here you are, presented with a suspect whose credentials are exemplary, and you're hesitating.'

'I know, I know, it's just that...'

'I'm listening,' said Munro. 'What's the problem?'

'Okay,' said West. 'Not only does she know Byrne and Jardine, she's also got a motive for doing them both in.'

'Agreed.'

'Plus, she's got a supply of Buprenorphine, and she knows how to handle a syringe.'

'Correct.'

'And she's wearing the same Sandalwood beads around her wrist that Byrne and Jardine had wrapped around theirs.'

'Well, if what she says is true,' said Munro, 'perhaps she placed them there in the hope it might bring them back from the brink.'

'Perhaps.'

'But?'

'Instinct,' said West. 'It's not her. She's too... nice. Too... peace, love and understanding.'

'What about the evidence, Charlie?' said Munro, playing devil's advocate. 'It's all stacked against her.'

'What evidence?' said West. 'It's all circumstantial. No matter how candid she's been with us, there's nothing to back it up. If we nicked her and she decided to change her story, we'd be screwed.'

'This might help,' said Munro as he reached into his pocket and pulled out a neatly folded length of toilet tissue.

'What's this?'

'Macallan's hair. I took it from the brush in the bathroom. If it matches the samples they took from Byrne's car, then you'll have something concrete to go on, no matter what she says.'

'You crafty sod,' said West. 'Thanks, but I'm still not buying it. Something doesn't feel right, and it's nothing to do with breakfast. What are you smirking at?'

'You, Charlie. You're finally dispensing with rational thought and following your heart.'

'Yeah, I'm not sure that's such a good thing.'

'You need instinct to catch a killer, Charlie. The facts are simply there to prove their guilt. The only question that remains is: where does that leave you, now?'

'Well, unless Craig Ferguson can tell us something we don't already know, then two words spring to mind: creek and paddle.'

Chapter 13

Unlike Munro, whose hatred of hospitals stemmed from a botched tonsillectomy at the age of eight and a spell in the ICU as the victim of a hit and run nearly sixty years later, West found the allure of surgeons in scrubs, and doctors doting on the sick and needy, an almost irresistible attraction.

With his hands clasped behind his back and his nose twitching at the pervasive smell of disinfectant, he followed her along the corridor and huffed impatiently as she paused by the vending machine for an over-priced bar of chocolate and a bottle of water.

'Lunchtime, Jimbo,' she said. 'Do you want anything?'

'Aye, but I'm not that desperate, lassie. I'll get something on the way out. The sooner the better.'

* * *

When she'd woken up dishevelled next to a man she didn't know, in a house she didn't recognise, with no recollection of the night before, Mary Jardine – realising she was on borrowed time – knew she had to make a choice: either end up in a body bag, or get a grip and sort her life out.

After cutting ties with the jakies and the junkies she had once called friends, and having had the temerity to book herself into rehab, she found herself a job and, though struggling with even the simplest of tasks as she went through a painful period of withdrawal, set herself on the road to recovery before succumbing to another source of dependency – namely Craig Ferguson – who offered her the security and stability she so desperately needed; ironically, two qualities sorely lacking in his own empty life.

Looking jaded and worn, she sat with her eyes closed, her head resting against the wall and the baby sleeping soundly in her lap.

'Alright?' she said, roused by the sound of footsteps in the corridor.

'Here you go,' said West, handing her the chocolate and the bottle of water, 'something to keep you going. This is James, by the way, we work together.'

Munro nodded politely as he took a seat beside her.

'That's a bonny wee bairn you've got there,' he said. 'Boy or a girl?'

'Boy. He's called Jamie.'

'I can think of no finer name. How are you, Mrs Ferguson?'

'Okay, considering. Actually, no. I'm shattered.'

'That's understandable, given the circumstances. You've not been here all night, have you?'

'No, no,' said Mary. 'I got a call this morning, much like yourselves, I imagine. Am I right?'

'Indeed you are.'

'I'm just waiting on the doctor, they said he'll not be long.'

'Listen, Mrs Ferguson,' said West, 'I need to ask a favour. Would you mind if we nipped in first? It's just that the sooner we can talk to Craig, the sooner we can get on. We won't be long.'

'Aye, no bother,' said Mary. 'Your need is greater than mine, I suppose. Are you any nearer yet? To finding out who did it?'

'Yeah, we're on the case,' said West, her eyes lighting up at the sight of the doctor heading towards them. 'We'll have him soon enough, don't you worry.'

* * *

At forty-four years old and looking as if he spent more time on the beach than he did in the stressed environment of the ICU, Ross Cockburn – wearing a pale blue tunic with a stethoscope draped around his neck – flashed a smile as he ran his fingers through his thick, black hair.

'Quite the welcoming party,' he said. 'That should cheer him up.'

'How is he?' said Ferguson.

'He's awake, he's lucid, and he's hungry. That's always a good sign. You're Mrs Ferguson, I presume?'

'I am, aye.'

'And you are?'

'DI West. And this is my colleague. We need to have a quick word with Craig, if that's alright.'

'Oh, I'm not sure about that,' said Cockburn. 'Family's one thing, but a whole heap of questions when he's just come off the…'

'You've seen the state he's in?'

'Aye, well of course, I have.'

'And would you rather the bloke responsible was out roaming the streets, or…'

'Point taken, Inspector,' said Cockburn, grinning. 'You're obviously a lady who gets what she wants.'

'You'd better believe it.'

'Okay. Five minutes. That's all.'

'Cheers.'

'And don't wind him up. If I hear any beeps from that monitor, that's you out on your ear. Do I make myself clear?'

'Crystal,' said West, smiling coyly. 'We'll behave ourselves. Promise.'

* * *

Lying on his back with a couple of tubes pumping him full of fluids and nutrients, and an assortment of wires attached to his fingers, arms, and chest, Craig Ferguson – looking like a live specimen in a laboratory experiment – turned his head and winced as Munro and West entered the room.

'Blimey,' she said. 'You look… colourful.'

'That'll be the bruising,' said Craig. 'Is it bad?'

'Have you seen a mirror?'

'Not yet.'

'Just as well. I'd give it a couple of weeks, if I were you.'

'Your bedside manner is second to none.'

'Sorry. Did I sound…?'

'No, you're alright,' said Craig. 'It makes a change. Everyone around here's so serious, it's like they expect me to die.'

'They probably do,' said Munro. 'Tell me Craig, are you familiar with the four horsemen of the apocalypse?'

'I am, aye.'

'Well, they're on the board of the NHS.'

'Oh, no jokes, please,' said Craig, 'it's too painful. So, who are you? I'm guessing, police?'

'In one,' said West. 'I'm DI West and this is James Munro. Do you feel up to answering a few questions? Nothing heavy.'

'Aye, okay.'

'Remember,' said Munro, 'you dinnae have to answer any if you'd prefer not to. And if you want us to leave, just make that machine beep a wee bit faster and the doctor will have us out of here in no time at all.'

'Okay,' said West. 'Let's start with a silly one: how are you feeling? You've been out cold for days.'

'Aye, so they say. I'm okay, I think. Just a wee bit sore, here and there.'

'And how's your memory?'

'Fine, so far. Are you wanting to put it to the test?'

'If you don't mind.'

'Fire away.'

'It's an obvious one, I know,' said West, 'but have you any idea who did this to you?'

'I know exactly who did this to me,' said Craig, grimacing as he tried to sit up. 'Sean. Sean Jardine.'

West, enthused by his answer, dragged a chair from the wall and sat beside the bed.

'And this was last Friday?' she said.

'It was definitely a Friday,' said Craig, 'but I can't say which one. How long have I been I here?'

'Not long. Do you remember what happened?'

'Aye, I do. He jumped me just around the corner from the pub, as I was heading for my car.'

'And do you know why?'

'We'd had a... disagreement. A wee... misunderstanding.'

'A wee misunderstanding?' said West. 'That's got to be the understatement of the year. Was it about the loan?'

'Loan?' said Craig. 'What loan?'

'Rona said...'

'You've spoken to Rona?'

'Of course. Is there a problem with that?'

'No, no,' said Craig. 'I'd just rather she wasn't involved, that's all.'

'Too late for that, I'm afraid. Now, she said you'd borrowed some money from Alan Byrne.'

'I did, aye.'

'Okay,' said West, 'so, as Alan Byrne and Sean Jardine were running a loan racket together, we just assumed…'

'Sorry,' said Craig, 'I don't mean to interrupt but Sean was running a loan racket?'

'You mean, you didn't know?'

'First I've heard of it.'

West, clearly perplexed, slumped back in her chair and folded her arms.

'Then what's all this about the money you borrowed?'

'A big deal over nothing, by the sounds of it,' said Craig. 'I used to bump into Alan in the pub after work.'

'So, you were mates?'

'I wouldn't go that far. Just a couple of punters having a beer together.'

'So?'

'So, I was strapped for cash one night and I tapped him for fifty quid. I never realised he was such a tight-arse. He kept hounding me to pay it back.'

West, even more confused, ruffled her hair in frustration.

'Fifty quid?' she said incredulously. 'You're sure about that?'

'Aye, positive. I should know, I'm the one who borrowed it. Why?'

'Rona got in touch with Byrne…'

'She did what?'

'…because she thought you were skint. She offered to pay your debt but Byrne told her you owed him fifty grand.'

Craig smiled and rolled his head against the pillow.

'No, no, no,' he said. 'That's ridiculous. He must have been joking her.'

'So, it wasn't fifty grand?'

'Fifty quid, Inspector. Straight up.'

'Then why would he say that?'

'Search me,' said Craig. 'Maybe he saw her as an easy touch.'

'Okay, hold on,' said West, taking a deep breath and frowning as she gathered her thoughts. 'Let's go back a bit. You lost your job a while back, is that right?'

'Aye, unfortunately, it is.'

'Gross misconduct?'

'Is that what they called it?'

'Do you mind telling us what happened?'

'Is it relevant?'

'Maybe.'

'If you'd rather not,' said Munro, standing by the door like an impartial observer at the ballot box, 'then you dinnae have to.'

'Oh, it's ancient history now, I suppose,' said Craig. 'We were having a party in the office, someone's birthday, and I'd had a few bevvies. One too many, if I'm honest. And I made a pass at the boss.'

'And she didn't like it?' said West.

Craig turned his head and smiled.

'He. He didn't like it.'

Munro, bewildered by her lack of perception, stared at West and rolled his eyes as he waited for the penny to drop.

'So, you're…gay?' she said.

'One hundred per cent, Inspector. Shocking, isn't it?'

'No. It isn't. I mean… but what about Rona? Weren't you and she having an affair?'

'In her dreams, maybe. No, no, I'm kidding. We're pals. Good pals. She might've fancied me at some point but after we'd been out a couple of times, I set her straight. She didn't even bat an eyelid. She said she thought our friendship was worth more than that and we've been friends ever since. We hang out together, we have a laugh.'

'I hate to ask,' said West. 'But what about Mary?'

Craig lay back and stared at the ceiling.

'Well, now,' he said with a sigh. 'That's a different story.'

'So, she doesn't know?'

'She has no idea. It's a subject I've yet to broach. No doubt it'll come out in the wash once the divorce gets rolling.'

'Rather you than me,' said West. 'Tell me to sod off if I'm prying, but why did you marry her if you knew you were gay?'

'I didn't,' said Craig. 'Not then. I knew something wasn't right but I couldn't put my finger on it. It's like... have you ever found yourself in a space you didn't want to be in? Despite everything being perfect on the outside?'

West glanced at Munro and lowered her head.

'Yup. But me almost marrying the wrong bloke is hardly the same.'

'It sounds exactly the same,' said Craig. 'See here, Inspector, we ticked all the right boxes: nice couple, nice house, nice car, and a bairn on the way; but there was one box we couldn't tick, the one marked "happy".'

Munro, aware that Craig had touched a nerve, interrupted proceedings with a swift change of subject as he noticed West's concentration beginning to lapse.

'If you dinnae mind me asking,' he said, 'how were you coping financially? I mean, it cannae be easy with a mortgage to pay and a bairn on the way.'

'Aye, you're not wrong there, Mr Munro. Sean was helping me out. He was slipping me a couple of grand each month until I got myself sorted.'

'Sean? But I thought you said you didn't have a loan with Sean?'

'I didn't.'

'By jiminy, now you're confusing me,' said Munro. 'What's a couple of grand a month, if it's not a loan?'

'I don't know,' said Craig. 'A gift? It's no different to say, a husband giving his wife some housekeeping.'

'What are you getting at?' said West. 'Sean didn't get on with his sister, so why would he suddenly bung you a couple of grand unless...'

'Well done, Inspector,' said Craig, smiling limply. 'You've caught up at last. Sean and I were... we were seeing each other.'

'Blimey,' said West. 'Talk about keep it in the family.'

'I know. Doesn't look good, does it? God knows how I'm going to tell Mary. Once she finds out, I'll be right back in here, that's for sure.'

'She might not have to,' said Munro, muttering under his breath.

West stood, returned the chair to the wall, and walked to the foot of the bed.

'Sorry, Craig,' she said, 'but I'm still a bit lost. If you and Sean were an item, and he was supporting you, then why the hell did he do this?'

'Rona,' said Craig. 'He found out I was seeing Rona and couldn't handle the fact that we were just pals. He thought I was playing him for a fool and sleeping with her behind his back. He got jealous.'

'The possessive kind, is he?'

'Very.'

'And he's got a temper.'

'Oh, he has that.'

'Just so you know, once he'd had a pop at you, he went after her.'

'He killed the goat, didn't he?'

'Yup.'

'I knew it. God, I've got some explaining to do when I get out.'

'Yeah, don't envy you that,' said West, 'but from what I've seen of Rona, she seems pretty cool. We'll let her know you're up and talking and she'll be down to see you soon, I'm sure. Listen, before we go... actually, no. We'll save it for next time.'

'No, you're alright,' said Craig. 'You've come this far, you may as well let me have it.'

'It's Alan Byrne,' said West. 'He's dead.'

'Oh, well,' said Craig. 'That's fifty quid in my pocket, then.'

'And I'm sorry to have to say this but… so is Sean.'

Craig closed his eyes and took a deep breath.

'Are you alright? It must be a shock, I know.'

'Not so much a shock,' said Craig. 'More a surprise. What was it?'

'Overdose.'

'Those bloody steroids! I told him to pack them in, but would he listen? No. Always had to play the big man.'

'It wasn't the steroids, Craig. We're pretty certain he was murdered.'

'Murdered? Are you joking me?

'No. Alan Byrne died just a few days earlier, same thing. There's probably a connection between the two.'

'Visiting time, eh?' said Craig. 'Whatever happened to a bunch of bananas and a bottle of Lucozade?'

'We'll leave you in peace.'

'Aye, okay. Listen, I don't suppose Mary…?'

'She's outside. We'll send her in. Oh, and you need to have a chat with her once you're home.'

'What about?'

'Sean. He was HIV positive.'

Chapter 14

With a face like a fisherman who'd failed to land his catch, and reeling from the revelation that Craig was spawning like a salmon with Sean Jardine, West – her confidence ebbing away – was floundering like a fish out of water.

'You couldn't make it up, could you?' she said, glancing at Munro as they strolled along the corridor. 'I mean, Craig Ferguson and Sean Jardine? Who'd have thought?'

'As they say, Charlie, the truth is often stranger than fiction. It's that lassie I feel sorry for, she's the one left holding the bairn.'

'Yeah, and I can't see her being too happy once she finds out what her husband's been up to. Nothing like a bit of infidelity to dent the ego.'

'Right enough,' said Munro, 'but he seems like a good lad, I cannae see him leaving her high and dry.'

'Maybe,' said West, 'but where does that leave me?'

'I don't know, Charlie. Where does that leave you?'

West stopped and turned to Munro with the woeful look of a vegan vacationing on a Venezuelan cattle ranch.

'I don't know, Jimbo,' she said. 'Honest to God, I really don't know.'

'Well, you've only got one suspect: Rona Macallan. I suggest you concentrate on her.'

West, hands in pockets, stared at the floor as they continued slowly towards reception.

'Alright, look,' she said, 'I admit, the evidence against her is pretty overwhelming and she's got no qualms about burying a goat or killing a chicken so I doubt topping a couple of blokes would make that much difference to her, but we've got nothing to prove it. Even if we get a match from the hair you filched from her bathroom, all that does is prove she was in Byrne's car, which she's admitted to, anyway. I'm just not convinced it's her.'

'Then stop trying to prove she's guilty, Charlie,' said Munro, 'and start trying to prove her innocence. Then you can eliminate her from the inquiry and start afresh.'

West stopped abruptly and spun to face Munro.

'You,' she said, grinning wildly, 'are a bloody genius! It's like reverse psychology!'

'Is it, indeed?'

'God, everything seems so much simpler, now! Okay, we need to cross-match the hair sample with the strands we got from Byrne's car. Then I need to bring her in and get a set of dabs, see if they match the unidentified set from Jardine's motor. And, while we're at it, we should see if we can lift any prints off the beads those two were wearing. It's got to be worth a look. And if we draw a blank, then bingo, she's off the hook.'

'Well done, Charlie,' said Munro, 'but have you not forgotten something?'

'Don't think so.'

'The car park by the McTurk bridge, is it still sealed off?'

'Yeah, of course. Why?'

'Because now that you know what killed Jardine, you'll be wanting a murder weapon. You need the SOCOs to do a clean sweep of the area, it'll be easier now that the weather's improved. Rubbish bins, drains, hedges, even the water under the bridge. It's a syringe you'll be looking for and mark my words, it'll not be easy to find.'

* * *

Apart from an elderly gent engrossed in The Herald, a forlorn-looking lady making enquiries at the desk, and a doctor chatting in hushed tones with a lady by the far window, the reception area was, unusually, all but deserted.

West froze and grabbed Munro by the sleeve as the doctor gently placed an arm around the young lady's shoulder and guided her towards them.

'Oh, crap!' she said, muttering under her breath.

'What is it, Charlie?' said Munro as he followed her line of sight, his face wrinkling as he smiled. 'Ah-ha! Your registrar friend, I assume?'

'Yes!'

'And he's with a dolly bird, too.'

'No need to rub it in. Oh, God, he's coming over. How do I get out of this?'

'Confrontation is the best way to overcome your fears, lassie. I'll be waiting in the car.'

West cursed through gritted teeth as Munro disappeared through the door, leaving her to face a beaming Doctor Bowen.

'Inspector!' he said. 'Nice to see you again. What brings you here?'

'Craig Ferguson,' said West, bluntly.

'The lad in the ICU?'

'Yup. He's up and about.'

'Oh, that is good news. I was hoping I'd see you.'

'Why's that?'

'Well, because last time we met, you seemed in an awful hurry to get away. I hope I didn't say anything to upset you?'

'Nah, I'm made of stronger stuff, no need to worry on that score.'

'That's alright, then,' said Bowen. 'Oh, where are my manners; Inspector, I'd like you meet my daughter Ally. Ally, this is Detective Inspector West.'

West's face dropped as her eyes flitted between the attractive, young girl and her father.

'Your daughter?' she said.

'Aye, of course,' said Bowen. 'Who did you...? Oh! Now, I get it! That explains everything!'

'I don't know what you mean.'

'Aye, you do! When we met and I said I was taking Ally for a spin on the bike, you thought I was talking about my wife!'

West lowered her gaze and kicked fluff from the carpet.

'It's possible,' she said, 'that I may have misconstrued what you meant, but...'

'Ally, would you give us a minute, sweetheart?'

Bowen waited while his daughter took a seat and lowered his voice.

'Your cheeks, Inspector, they're quite the shade of pink all of a sudden.'

'Hot flush,' said West. 'Must be the chilli I had for breakfast.'

'Aye, chilli for breakfast. Does it every time. So, how are you?'

'Fine. Oh, look, I'm sorry, okay. It was my fault, I shouldn't have jumped to conclusions.'

'No, no, it's me,' said Bowen. 'I should've said.'

'Well, no harm done, eh? So, how about you? Are you alright?'

'Oh, aye. Much better, now. And just for the record, my wife and I separated years ago. Ally stops with me. She's at uni.'

'You don't have to explain.'

'Oh, I think I do. I wouldn't want to go through that again, especially if you've changed your mind about that ride on the bike.'

West, playing an unconvincing game of hard-to-get, bit her lip and frowned.

'Maybe,' she said. 'Yeah, why not. It might be fun.'

'Good,' said Bowen. 'I'm on lates all week so I'm free in the afternoons. When do you fancy? Tomorrow, maybe?'

'Okay,' said West. 'As long as it's not plopping down, you're on.'

* * *

West slipped silently into the passenger seat and fastened her safety belt as Munro, catching sight of the smug expression smeared across her face, shook his head and smiled.

'Looks like I'll have to find myself somewhere else to stay,' he said. 'I'll not play gooseberry to a couple of turtle doves.'

'Don't be daft,' said West with a grin. 'You'll do nothing of the sort.'

'I'm a light sleeper, Charlie. I'm not keen on things that go bump in the night.'

'You'll feel a bump on the back of your head if you don't shut it. The office please, James. And don't spare the horses.'

* * *

'Have you eaten, Dougal?'

'Not yet, miss. I'm famished.'

'Then it's your lucky day,' said West as she placed two small, thin-crust pizzas on the desk. 'One's pepperoni and peppers, the other's basically a lump of dough with some cheese on the top.'

'As it should be,' said Munro as he swiped a slice.

'No sign of Duncan?'

'He's away to see the French fella, miss,' said Dougal. 'He'll not be long. Did you get yourselves to the hospital?'

'We did, indeed,' said Munro, 'and Craig Ferguson was singing like a canary.'

'And how about Rona Macallan?'

'I'm glad you asked me that,' said West. 'Because we need to bring her in, as soon as possible. Can you sort it, please?'

'Aye, no bother. What's the story?'

'In a nutshell, everything's against her. She admits to being with Byrne with his motor, she knew about Craig Ferguson's loan which... long story, I'll tell you later; more to the point, she has her own stock of 'prenorphine.'

'Jeez-oh! Why would she have that?'

'For the ponies, apparently,' said West as she handed him the wad of toilet tissue. 'We need this tested, it's her hair and it'll probably match the samples from Byrne's car, and we need her prints, too.'

'So, are we going to charge her?'

'Nope.'

'No? Why not?'

'Because she didn't do it.'

Dougal dusted down his fingers, returned to his desk, and flipped his laptop round to face them.

'I've got something that might change your mind,' he said as he played a grainy, black and white video. 'Look at this.'

'Riveting,' said Munro, staring at the fuzzy image on the screen. 'What is it, exactly?'

'CCTV from the camera outside the community hospital, boss. It's directed at the entrance so it doesn't capture the road as such, just enough to see the cars go by.'

'Well, so far we've seen two cars, a bike, and a pedestrian,' said West as she reached for another slice of pizza. 'Can't we watch Netflix, instead?'

'Hold on,' said Dougal as he slowed the playback. 'Here. That's Jardine's car, and he's travelling towards the Keir McTurk bridge.'

'Brilliant,' said West, 'but that's where we found him, so what's the big deal?'

Dougal fast-forwarded eleven minutes and thirty-eight seconds and stopped the tape.

'That,' he said, tapping the screen, 'is a Land Rover Defender. It's Rona Macallan's Defender.'

The room fell silent as West – oblivious to the watchful gaze of an amused Munro – left her seat and, deep in thought, slowly paced the floor like a counsel for the defence seeking an explanation for her client's incriminating behaviour.

'How much of that tape have you watched?' she said, without looking up.

'About ninety minutes on from here, miss. That takes us well beyond the point the first responders arrived at the scene.'

'And you didn't notice anyone else travelling in the same direction? I mean, anyone unusual? Anyone speeding?'

'Nothing out of the ordinary, miss. No.'

West stopped, raised her head, and smiled.

'How about coming back?'

'Excuse me?'

'Did you see Macallan's Defender coming back?'

'Actually, no,' said Dougal, becoming flustered.

'Well, if she's guilty,' said West, 'if she did nobble Jardine, then she'd be coming back along the same road no more than say, fifteen, twenty minutes later, wouldn't she?'

'Aye, she would. Unless she went another way.'

'And is there another way?'

Dougal slumped in his chair and sighed.

'No, not really,' he said. 'Not if she was heading home.'

'Then maybe she was going somewhere else.'

'At that time of night?'

'Oh, come on, Dougal,' said West. 'It wasn't that late. Blimey, the pubs were still open.'

Munro polished off his pizza, finished his tea, and regarded West with a look of satisfaction.

'Well done, Charlie,' he said. 'Keep this up and you'll be enjoying a career change before long.'

'How do you mean?'

'Charlotte West. QC.'

'Very funny.'

'So, will I bring her in, now?' said Dougal.

'No, no,' said Munro, 'it's too late for that. Give her a wee call, ask her to drop by tomorrow. Tell her it's just a formality, she'll understand. And it'll give her time to tend to her flock so she's not fretting while she's away.'

'Right you are, boss.'

'Oh, and Dougal,' said West, 'we need to send SOCOs back to the car park. Somewhere around there is the syringe that was used to kill Jardine and we need to find it.'

* * *

Standing in the doorway like a destitute gunslinger in a wild west saloon, Duncan – needing only a poncho, and a cheroot dangling from his lip to complete the picture – scanned the room and scowled as his eyes settled on the empty boxes.

'Now that,' he said, 'is the definition of disappointment.'

'What is?' said West.

'Being tempted by the smell of pizza only to find there's none left.'

'Never mind, it's nearly home time,' said West. 'You can treat yourself to a kebab after the pub.'

'Aye, you're right. That trumps a Margherita any day of the week.'

'How'd you get on?'

'Foubert?' said Duncan as he slouched in a chair and cocked his feet on the desk. 'Nice fella, right enough, which is surprising in itself.'

'How come?'

'Because you wouldn't think it if you saw him. He's got the look of a psychopath and a face like a spud that's gone ten rounds with Rocky Marciano.'

'So, apart from his deceptive features,' said West, 'what did he have to say for himself?'

'He reckons he only knew Byrne and Jardine to chat to in the lift, and he certainly didn't socialise with them on account of the fact that he doesn't drink.'

'Utter tosh,' said Munro. 'A Frenchman who doesnae drink? That's like saying Italians dinnae care for pasta.'

'Either way, I need to corroborate his story with his co-workers,' said Duncan. 'I also took a look at his phone and, not only does he not have either of their numbers in his list of contacts, but he'd also deleted his call history.'

'He thinks he's being clever,' said West, smirking. 'But we're one step ahead of him. We know for a fact that Jardine called him several times just before he copped it.'

'Shall we have him in for a formal chat?'

'Let's get some ammunition on our side first,' said West, reaching for her coat. 'Have a word with his colleagues and see what you can come up with. Then, see if he's self-employed like Jardine, if not, get a record of all his payslips and any bonuses he's had…'

'Roger that.'

'…then, Dougal, take a crafty look at his bank account and see if it all tallies.'

'No bother. Is that you away?'

'Yup. I need to check out some biker gear.'

* * *

Without an inquisitive wife to monitor his every move, Munro – left to his own devices – steered his way around the kitchen like a Michelin-starred chef, dicing-up a chunk of thick-cut rump, slicing carrots, rolling-out pastry and peeling potatoes in between sampling the Balvenie which, much to his annoyance, seemed to be evaporating at a rate of knots due to West's new-found fondness for a nightcap or two.

With supper in the oven, the spuds on the hob, and a glass of wine in hand, he settled in front of the laptop intent on browsing some property porn, when his viewing pleasure was interrupted by the arrival of West who blundered through the door like a contestant on Supermarket Sweep.

'Bloody hell,' she said, dumping the bags on the floor. 'Pour me one of those, would you? I'm parched.'

'That's an awful lot of shopping,' said Munro. 'Were you panic buying or simply exhibiting the female side of your nature?'

'That's so sexist.'

'I do my best.'

'I got distracted in the food hall,' said West as she pulled a waxed-cotton jacket from one of the bags and held it to her chest. 'What do you think? It's a Belstaff. It's warm and it's waterproof, so it will do for work as well a ride on the back of a bike.'

'Very smart, Charlie,' said Munro as he handed her a glass. 'It reminds me of one I used to wear as a young man, terrorising the folk of Dumfries on my Triumph.'

'You used to be a biker?'

'In a manner of speaking. Traffic. Two years.'

'Well, well. I wonder what other secrets you've got hidden up your sleeve?'

'None you need know about.'

West sat down and sipped her wine while Munro, still in his apron, removed supper from the oven and started dishing up.

'Steak pie,' he said, placing the plates on the table. 'And it's homemade, I'll have you know.'

'That does it,' said West as she shovelled a steaming forkful into her mouth. 'You can't move out now. I won't allow it. So, what have you been up to? Apart from practising for Masterchef?'

'I've been looking at houses.'

'But you've already got a house.'

'Not for me,' said Munro. 'For you. You said you wanted a wee house with a garden so, as I had some time on my hands, I thought I'd take a look.'

'Nice one. Did you find anything?'

'Not yet, but I'll keep looking. So, what are your plans for tomorrow?'

'A little face-to-face with Macallan first,' said West. 'Dougal said she's dropping by about nine.'

'And you're sticking to your guns?'

'Yup. Despite everything, I bet she's got a watertight alibi which means she'll be off the hook.'

'I hope for your sake you're right, Charlie, even if it does mean you're left without a suspect.'

'I'll find one, don't you worry.'

'And then?'

'Then I'm nipping out for a quick threesome,' said West. 'Me, Doctor Bowen, and Fat Bob.'

Munro, his old-fashioned values leaving him ill-equipped to deal with such an outlandish comment, coughed and spluttered as he choked on his pie.

'Fat Bob!' said West, giggling hysterically. 'That's his bike! It's a Harley Davidson. It's called a Fat Bob!'

Taking a large sip of wine, Munro, regaining his composure, allowed himself a wry smirk.

'God bless Americans,' he said. 'Blunt and to the point, as ever. If it was a British bike, no doubt we'd refer to Bob as corpulent, or well-upholstered. Aye, that's the word – well-upholstered.'

Chapter 15

Beleaguered by man's obsession with hate and despairing of civilisation's quest to annihilate one another because of colour, creed, or for being a Hibs supporter, Rona Macallan – who firmly believed that tolerance and compassion held the key to existing without conflict – had long since preferred the company of animals whose symbiotic existence saw them resolve their differences with a gentle nudge or a simple peck on the ear rather than a broken jaw or the deployment of cruise missiles.

As an only child raised on the tenet that honesty was the best policy, a principle that only once fell short of its promise when she freely admitted to speeding along the A75 – an act of candour which, without the aid of a solicitor, landed her with four penalty points and a three-hundred-pound fine – believed, nonetheless, that deceit of any kind would ultimately result in a bad bout of karma.

Dabbing her fingertips with a wet-wipe, she sat quietly humming to herself in the still surroundings of the interview room while she waited for someone to arrive.

'Morning!' said West cheerily, as she flew through the door. 'Thanks for coming by, Miss Macallan, I know it's a bit out of your way so we'll try to keep it as brief as possible.'

'No problem,' said Macallan. 'Mr Munro, nice you see you again.'

'Likewise, I'm sure,' said Munro. 'Has anyone offered you a cup of tea? Or some coffee, perhaps?'

'No, you're alright. I'm fine, thanks.'

'I see you've had your prints done.'

'I have. Although, I must admit I'm a wee bit confused. Why would you need my fingerprints?'

'It's quite simple,' said West. 'You see, we found a set of prints on Sean Jardine's car which we can't identify, so we just need to make sure that they don't belong to you.'

'Oh, I could've told you that myself.'

'I'm sure you could,' said Munro, 'but unfortunately in our line of work, someone's word isn't always their bond.'

'I get that, right enough,' said Macallan. 'So, apart from that, what else can I help you with?'

'It's literally just a couple of questions,' said West. 'Don't take them personally, it's just stuff we need to ask.'

'I understand.'

'Okay, let's start with the Vetergesic you use to treat the colic; where do you get it from?'

'The surgery. On Townhead Street.'

'And is it by prescription?'

'No, no,' said Macallan, shaking her head. 'You can't get it willy-nilly, even with a prescription, only the vet can give it, to the animal, that is.'

'Then, would you mind explaining how you managed to get your hands on it?'

'Oh, that's easy. Colin, he's the vet, he and I have known each other for years. If I've ever needed some to treat the ponies, he's been kind enough to let me have it.'

'Is that allowed?'

'Kind of.'

'And how many times has he done this?' said West.

'Twice.'

154

'And the time before this?'

'Now, you're asking,' said Macallan. 'Must be a year ago. At least.'

'And how much of the stuff do you have?'

'At home? None. Not now.'

'So, you don't have bottles of it stockpiled in the shed?'

'No, that would be wrong,' said Macallan. 'I get just what I need, enough for a couple of jabs, preloaded in a syringe. That's it.'

Munro, one hand on his chin, regarded Macallan with an inquisitive smile.

'Tell me,' he said, 'if you happened to give a pony the whole dose in one go, by mistake I mean, what effect what would that have?'

'Nothing major,' said Macallan. 'It'll make him drowsier than normal, that's for sure, but he'd be fine.'

'So, it wouldnae kill him?'

'Good heavens, no. You'd need a bottleful to do that, if not more.'

'Yeah, I suppose so,' said West. 'After all, it is a horse we're talking about. What about you? What would happen if you took it?'

'Me? Are you asking: would it kill me? I really don't know. I'm sure you'd not need as much as you would to kill a horse, but how much exactly is anyone's guess.'

'Good,' said West confidently. 'Moving on. The other night you were driving along Ayr Road, past the community hospital. It was hacking down. Do you remember?'

'Aye, of course!' said Macallan. 'But how on earth did you know that?'

'We have our sources,' said Munro. 'Nothing to worry about, there's nothing sinister about it, I assure you.'

'I hope not.'

'Do you mind telling us where you were going?' said West.

'I was on my way to the supermarket.'

'The supermarket?'

'Aye. I never have time to go during the day so I tend to nip over in the evening. It's dead quiet then, too.'

'I know it's a bit much to ask,' said West, 'but can you prove you were actually there?'

'Prove it?' said Macallan as she rummaged through her pockets. 'Well, I've a cupboard full of groceries if that will do, apart from… oh, hold on – here. It's the receipt. That has the date and the time on it, does it not?'

'It does indeed,' said Munro. 'And just for the record, did you come back the same way?'

'No, I couldn't get by. There were police all over the road. I had to go round the houses to get home.'

'Well, apologies if it seems like we've given you the third degree, Miss Macallan, but we cannae leave any stone unturned, you understand?'

'It's fine, Mr Munro, really. Is that you done, now?'

'It is.'

'Then, I'll see myself out. Give me a ring if you need anything else.'

* * *

West, not given to patting herself on the back, glanced at Munro with a portentous look on her face.

'Like I said, Jimbo,' she said, trying not to sound too smug, 'she's got a watertight alibi.'

'I'm afraid it's sprung a leak, lassie.'

'What? How?'

'Rona Macallan could easily have stopped off at the car park and given Jardine a wee jab before continuing on her way to the supermarket.'

'Yes, but she didn't have enough 'prenorphine on her to do the job, did she?'

'You're forgetting what your friend the pathologist said, Charlie.'

'Which was?'

'Which was,' said Munro, 'that he didn't have a fatal dose of Buprenorphine in his body. That he keeled over because of the effect it had on the dire state of his internal organs.'

'Well, call me stubborn if you like…'

'I'll stick with Taurean, somehow it sounds less offensive.'

'…but I still think she's innocent.'

West stood, fastened the belt around her new jacket, and paused by the door.

'Are you… are you in a rush to get your lunch? Or are you heading upstairs to the office?'

Munro's steely, blue eyes sparkled knowingly as he stared at West.

'What are you after, Charlie?'

'Nothing. I just wondered if you fancied giving me a lift to my ménage à trois. That's all.'

* * *

Munro pulled up by the entrance to the hospital, lowered the visor against the glaring sun, and turned to West like an anxious father dropping his daughter at the senior prom.

'Lunch is an hour, Charlie. Dinnae get waylaid by the promise of a pint and a ploughman's, and make sure you hold the grab rail behind the seat, it's safer than clinging on to the rider, do I make myself clear?'

'Yes, Dad.'

'And when you're into a turn, lean with the bike, dinnae fight to stay upright, have you got that?'

'Yes, Dad.'

'Will I wait for you?'

'Don't be silly,' said West as she opened the door. 'He's got a bike, remember? I'll get him to drop me at the station.'

'As you wish, lassie. As you wish.'

'Are you heading straight back?'

157

'Aye,' said Munro. 'I'll just text Laurel and Hardy and see if they want some lunch. As I'm now a taxi driver, I may as well double-up as Uber Eats.'

'You're all heart,' said West. 'See you in an hour.'

* * *

Bowen, clad in his oil-stained jeans and a vintage leather jacket, smiled broadly as West wandered through reception.

'We've got the weather on our side,' he said. 'It must be an omen.'

'If it's anything like the film, you're going to need my stab vest. How are you?'

'Absolutely fine. I thought we could take a blast up to Ardrossan and grab a wee bite to eat.'

'Sounds perfect,' said West. 'Nothing fancy, I've only been let out for an hour.'

'No danger,' said Bowen as he handed her a crash helmet. 'I was only thinking burger and chips. Here, try this for size.'

West unpinned her hair and tucked the tresses into her collar as Bowen, distracted by a figure hovering by the door, patted her gently on the shoulder.

'Two ticks,' he said.

West, fastening the strap under her chin, locked eyes with the suited stranger and froze in a moment of vague recognition as Bowen shook his hand and ushered him outside.

Whipping off the helmet, she yanked the phone from her hip and frantically dialled the office.

'Duncan!'

'Aye, miss, what's up?'

'That Foubert bloke, what does he look like?'

'A thug,' said Duncan. 'Tall, five-eleven or thereabouts, and he's as bald as a coot with a map of Africa on his head.'

Dispensing with niceties, West hung up and called Munro.

'Jimbo!' she said. 'Where are you?'

'Car park, Charlie. Whatever is the matter?'

'Big bloke outside. Dark suit, looks like Gorbachev.'

'Aye, got him.'

'I think that's Claude Foubert. Get his registration and tell Dougal I want him picked up, now!'

'Nae bother, Charlie. Are you okay?'

'Yeah, yeah. Just get him picked up. I'll see you in an hour.'

* * *

Bowen, befuddled if not scared by West's fierce expression, apologised profusely.

'I am so sorry, Charlotte,' he said. 'Just a wee bit of business I had to attend to. So, will we go?'

'No,' said West, sternly. 'I think we need to have a chat first.'

'A chat?' What about?'

'Claude Foubert.'

'You've lost me,' said Bowen. 'Who's Claude Foubert?'

'The bloke you were just talking to.'

'Was it? Sorry, but I don't know his name, I just…'

'Just what?'

'It's nothing,' said Bowen sheepishly. 'It's personal.'

West took half a step back, drew herself up, and folded her arms.

'How much do you owe him?' she said, glowering.

Bowen glanced over his shoulder and sighed.

'Shall we go somewhere a little less public?'

Bowen hung his helmet on the wing mirror, perched sideways on the seat, and looked at West like a castigated schoolboy.

'I was desperate,' he said. 'Twenty-six grand a year for a ninety-hour week, a mortgage to pay and Ally to look after. It's not easy with the fees, and once term starts again, there's also her digs to pay for.'

'Digs?' said West. 'I thought she was staying with you?'

'Only during the holidays. She's at Durham, two years into a three-year BSc in Bioscience.'

'Look, I'm not having a go,' said West, 'and I'm not asking you to justify yourself to me, I just need to know what the score is, okay?'

'I got a loan.'

'Who from?'

'A fella called Byrne. One of the nurses gave me his number, she said he'd help me out.'

'Hold on. One of the nurses?'

Oh, aye. I'm not the only numpty in it up to my neck. There's a fair few of us here.'

'And?'

'And what?' said Bowen. 'That's it. I get a phone call saying Byrne's no longer coming to collect the payments and I should expect this other fella instead.'

'Foubert?'

'If you say so.'

West shoved her hands into her pockets and walked a circle, scuffing her heels as she went.

'You do know that that kind of racket is completely illegal, don't you?'

'Aye, of course, I do,' said Bowen. 'But what are the options for the likes of us? See here, Charlotte, I can't get an extension on the mortgage and the bank won't give me what I need. The bottom line is, I'll not have Ally finish uni with a massive debt hanging over her head. It's not right.'

'Rock and a hard place, eh?'

'Something like that.'

West looked to the sky and sighed.

'God, we had it easy, didn't we? Free education, I mean.'

'No,' said Bowen. 'We got what we were entitled to. I believe it's our duty to educate the kids, they shouldn't have to pay for it.'

'I won't argue with that. So, how much do you owe him?'

'Enough.'

'Look on the bright side,' said West as she zipped her coat. 'You might not have to pay it back.'

'How so?'

'Let's just say I've got a feeling you won't be seeing Foubert for quite some time. Shall we go?'

* * *

Anticipating what he regarded to be a just reward for instigating the swift apprehension of Claude Foubert, Dougal – his patience teetering on the edge of endurance as the clockwork timer wound its way down to zero – smiled with relief as Munro finally lifted the ham and cheese sandwiches from the toaster with the pizzazz of a magician pulling a rabbit from a hat.

'Dinnae sit there gawping,' he said. 'Somebody put the kettle on.'

'I'll do it,' said Duncan. 'Can we not wangle a toaster like that on expenses, chief?'

'You'll have to ask, Charlie,' said Munro. 'Decision-making's not a part of my remit anymore.'

'You don't know how lucky you are,' said West as she trudged through the door and flung herself at a chair.

'You're back early,' said Munro. 'Not a lovers' tiff, I hope?'

'I wasn't in the mood, that's all.'

'You were when I dropped you off. What happened?'

'Something came up.'

'You mean Foubert?'

'Yup. One of those for me?'

'Did you not have yourself some lunch?'

'Yeah, burger and chips. So?'

'Nothing, lassie. Here, help yourself.'

'So,' said West, 'did you get Foubert?'

'We did, miss,' said Dougal. 'He's downstairs ready for questioning.'

'Good. And did you manage to dig up anything concrete we can use against him?'

'Aye. Basically, he's running a similar set-up to Jardine but instead of being registered as a self-employed individual, he's down as CEO of a risk management consultancy that's registered in Paris. The company account is with HSBC on the Rue de Rivoli, that's where the money goes when his invoices are settled, then huge chunks are syphoned off to an account on the Isle of Man.'

'God, you have been busy.'

'Tell her about the other bit,' said Duncan. 'The withdrawals.'

'Oh, aye,' said Dougal, 'at first sight, there's nothing out of the ordinary. I can tell you where he eats, where he drinks, and where he shops because he uses a debit card for almost every transaction, but he also makes a lot of cash withdrawals.'

'Well, we all do that,' said West. 'How else would we get by?'

'These are over-the-counter cash withdrawals, miss. By prior arrangement. Nothing less than a couple of grand, two or three times a month.'

'Blooming heck,' said West, 'he must be earning a fortune.'

'He is.'

'Alright for some.'

'I was thinking,' said Duncan, 'maybe he's got some kind of a habit? Not drugs, it's too much cash for that, but gambling, maybe?'

'No, no,' said Munro. 'I'd wager the cash is for the punters queuing up to take advantage of his competitive interest rates.'

'I agree,' said West, 'we need to get him out of circulation as soon as possible. Dougal, you know his entire background, why don't you do the honours?'

'You want me to interview him?'

'Why not? But take Duncan with you, he looks a bit scary, it might loosen him up a bit.'

'Thanks very much,' said Duncan, handing her a mug. 'Here's your tea.'

Munro, serving himself last, as usual, sat at the desk, tucked a tea towel into his collar and glanced at West.

'So, come on, Charlie,' he said, biting into his toastie. 'What's the story?'

'Huh?'

'Did you not enjoy your sightseeing trip?'

'Sightseeing?' said West. 'I couldn't see a bloody thing, his head was in the way. In fact, I think I've cricked my neck.'

'That's not it.'

'No. It isn't. It's Byrne. And Jardine. And Foubert. The lot of them. Do you know, they've got half the flipping hospital in their pockets?'

'That, sadly, is not in the least bit surprising,' said Munro. 'Folk like that prey on the weak and the desperate.'

'But it's so unfair,' said West. 'All those nurses and doctors, they earn a pittance for what they do, so the upshot is that they have to resort to black market loans just to get by.'

'They're not the only ones, lassie. There's the firefighters too, and the teachers, and the social workers, and…'

'Yeah, alright, I get the picture. It still makes me mad, though. I mean, I know we don't earn a fortune, but we're not saving people's lives, are we?'

'That's debateable, Charlie,' said Munro. 'Correct me if I'm wrong, but I get the distinct impression that your outburst on the topic of social inequality has something to do with your registrar friend.'

'It has everything to do with my registrar friend. He's one of them.'

'You mean he's in hock to Foubert, as well?' said Dougal.

'He's in it up to his neck,' said West. 'I feel sorry for him. He only borrowed the cash so his daughter wouldn't be lumbered with a massive debt when she leaves uni. To be honest, he's so skint, I'm surprised he can afford to keep that bike on the road.'

West, looking as though she'd inadvertently swallowed a lump of tofu, slowly raised her arm and clicked her fingers at Dougal.

'That tape,' she said. 'The tape from outside the community hospital. Get it up.'

Dougal spun the laptop round to show the footage already paused on Macallan's Defender.

'Here we go, miss, this is where…'

'No, no, no!' said West impatiently. 'Go back. Go back to where you started from yesterday.'

'Okay, but there's nothing much apart from…'

'There!' said West. 'A car… then another…'

'Aye,' said Dougal, 'and in a minute that fella will walk by…'

'Stop! The bike! Can you zoom in a bit?'

Munro stood behind West, hands clasped firmly behind his back, and squinted at the screen.

'Why the fascination with the motorcycle, Charlie?'

She turned to face him with a look of desolation on her face.

'It's only a bleeding Harley, Jimbo. That's Fat Bob.'

* * *

Reaching for the evidence bag, West rummaged through its contents like someone who'd mistakenly tossed their lotto ticket into the waste paper basket before producing the white envelope stuffed with cash that she'd plucked from Jardine's jacket pocket.

'Look,' she said. 'NHS on the front. Return address: University Hospital.'

'Jeez-oh,' said Dougal. 'Are you saying the fella on the Harley is your registrar pal?'

'I don't know, but it's starting to look that way.'

She delved into the bag for a second time and fished out a clear, plastic pouch containing the leather glove found beneath the passenger seat of the BMW.

'You wouldn't wear these unless you owned a bike.'

Dougal grabbed the laptop and zoomed in even further.

'Miss,' he said. 'Your pal, he's only wearing one glove.'

'Just my luck.'

'So, what will you do now?' said Munro.

'Only one thing we can do. Duncan, bring him in.'

Chapter 16

After years of struggling to keep his head above water, Mark Bowen had every right to feel angry when his wife of seventeen years, who divided her time between the café at the gym and the local wine bar, hit him with the cliché: "it's not you, it's me", citing boredom as the reason for leaving what she deemed to be a loveless marriage.

Reminding her of the fact that she'd never worked a day in her life nor contributed anything towards the running of the household, he pointed her in the direction of the job centre and wished her on her way with a simple "on you go" and "don't forget to stay in touch".

Despite the turmoil of their separation and the pressure of working fourteen hour shifts in the volatile environment of the A&E, he refrained, unlike many of colleagues, from turning to alcohol as a way of alleviating the anger and the stress he'd kept bottled up inside him – an avoidance tactic which left him close to tipping point.

Declining the offer of a seat, he paced the floor grinding his teeth and muttering under his breath while Duncan, concerned he might blow a fuse at any point, remained on his feet should he need to intervene.

West entered the room, glanced at Bowen, and quietly closed the door behind her.

'Sorry,' she said as she pulled up a chair.

'Sorry?' said Bowen. 'Sorry? Is that it?'

'It's just routine, I need to…'

'Routine? You call arresting me on suspicion of murder, routine? Would a simple phone call not have sufficed?'

'No.'

'Or a polite invitation to have a wee chat? Was it really that necessary to send one of your officers to arrest me in front of the whole department?'

'Calm down and take a seat!'

'I will not calm down! I'm raging! Just who the hell am I supposed to have killed?'

'I said sit!'

Duncan took a step forward and nodded at the chair.

'Thanks,' said West as Bowen, glowering with contempt, reluctantly complied. 'This isn't easy for me either, you know.'

'Oh, spare me the self-pity, Charlotte!'

'Look, there's some stuff that's come to light and I need to get to the bottom of it, alright? Now, do you want a solicitor?'

'Why would I want a solicitor?'

'I can appoint one, if you'd like.'

'What I'd like is for you to tell me what the hell you're playing at!'

West, her eyes narrowing as her patience wore thin, stared at Bowen and stabbed the voice recorder.

'DI West,' she said. 'The time is 4.17 p.m. Also present is DC Duncan Reid. For the benefit of the tape, would you please state your name.'

'Bowen. Doctor Mark Bowen.'

'Good. Doctor Bowen…'

'How very formal.'

'…do you know a Mr Alan Byrne?'

'No,' said Bowen. 'I have *met* a Mr Alan Byrne. But I do not *know* a Mr Alan Byrne.'

'Well, I'm glad we've cleared that up. How did you meet?'

'Through a mutual acquaintance.'

'And why did you contact him?'

'To arrange a loan.'

'Would you mind telling us how much it was?'

'Aye. I would. I'd mind very much, indeed.'

'Did you meet Mr Byrne on more than one occasion?'

'I did.'

'And why was that?' said West.

'He was collecting the repayments on the loan.'

'Did you ever deal with any of his associates?'

'Aye,' said Bowen. 'The French fella. You know his name.'

'For the benefit of the tape Doctor Bowen is referring to Claude Foubert. How many times did you meet?'

'Twice.'

'So, you've never met anyone called Sean Jardine?'

'I've never even heard of him.'

'Then perhaps,' said West as she leaned back and folded her arms, 'you'd care to explain what you were doing in his car?'

'You've lost me.'

'Cumnock. Ayr Road car park. Blue BMW.'

'Oh, the blue BMW!' said Bowen breaking into laughter. 'You mean the dead fella! Okay, so that's what this is about, is it?'

'He was murdered.'

'Was he indeed?'

'And so was Alan Byrne.'

'And you think I was behind it?'

'Look,' said West, 'we're simply following a lead, that's all.'

Bowen, unable to contain himself, smiled broadly and jabbed a finger in her direction.

'Do you keep a wee sponge in that bag of yours, Charlotte?'

'A sponge?'

'Aye, because you'll be needing one to wipe the egg off your face once we're done here.'

Duncan, trying his best not to laugh, turned away as West stood up, tucked her chair beneath the desk, and leant against the wall.

'So,' she said. 'The car park. What were you doing there?'

'I was on my way to collect Ally.'

'You're telling me she was waiting for you in a dingy car park, in the middle of the night, in the pouring rain?'

'No. I never said that, did I? Ally had been doing some research at the Baird Institute all day and after that she went for a wee drink with her friend. I pulled in to call her to find out which pub she was in.'

'So you stopped there instead of pulling up on the road?'

'Oh, come on,' said Bowen, 'you've travelled that road yourself. It's too narrow to stop. I'd have caused a hold-up if I didn't get walloped up the backside.'

'And what happened next?

'What do you think? I called Ally. She was at the Craighead Inn.'

'And then?'

'And then,' said Bowen, 'I noticed the fella in the car.'

'In the dark?'

'Aye. The door wasn't shut properly, the light was on. I could see him as clear as day.'

'So, you went over?'

'Of course I did!' said Bowen. 'I'm a doctor and the fella didn't look as if he'd stopped for a nap. He was still warm, I checked for a pulse and there was none. I figured cardiac so I sent for an ambulance and I told them not to bother with the paramedics because he was dead. Oh, and I sent for you lot, too.'

'And that was it?'

'You want more?'

'You didn't hang around?'

'I told you,' said Bowen. 'I had to collect my daughter. I gave control my name, and my address, and my telephone number, and I told them to contact me if they wanted anything else but I've not heard from anyone, okay?'

'Okay,' said West. 'I need your permission to check your phone.'

'Why?'

'To verify your calls.'

'Feel free.'

'Where is it?'

'They took it,' said Bowen. 'Your pals. Along with my fingerprints, my wallet, my keys, and my dignity.'

West glanced at Duncan.

'They're running a match on the prints now,' he said.

West, head bowed and hands in pockets, pushed herself off the wall and began a circuit of the room.

'Why did you open the passenger door,' she said, 'when he was sitting in the driver's seat?'

'Because there was a car parked alongside and it was too close to get it open.'

'I see. Guess what we found under the seat.'

'The ark of the covenant.'

'One of your gloves.'

'Good. I was wondering where that went.'

'So, you admit it's yours?'

'I hope it's mine. They're not cheap.'

'Why did you take it off?'

'Have you tried dialling a phone with a glove on?'

Disappointed by Bowen's display of veracity, West, beginning to fear she'd jumped the gun for a second time, paused as she pondered her next question.

'You say you've no idea who the bloke in the car was, right?'

170

'Nothing wrong with your memory, is there?'

'And you'd never met?'

'Correct.'

'Then can you explain why he was carrying an envelope in his breast pocket? An NHS envelope, from the hospital?'

'Perhaps it was a letter telling him he had something terminal.'

'It was stuffed with cash,' said West.

'So, what do you want me to do about it?'

'You didn't give it to him?'

'Your memory's okay,' said Bowen, 'but you're obviously going deaf. I've already told you, I gave my money to the French fella. That envelope could've come from anyone.'

West returned to her seat and stared across the desk at Bowen, keen to note even the slightest facial giveaway as she delivered her final question.

'How'd you get hold of the 'prenorphine?' she said.

Bowen cocked his head and frowned.

'What on earth are you talking about?

'Alan Byrne and Sean Jardine were both killed by a fatal dose of Buprenorphine.'

'Oh, and because I'm a doctor, you think that makes me a likely suspect? Well, listen hen, if anyone came to the hospital in need of Buprenorphine, they'd not come to me, they'd be heading for the ICU.'

'It's a hospital, you could've got your hands on it, somehow.'

'Oh, that's right. I'll tell you what I did, shall I? I sneaked over to Oncology, jimmied open the store, and nicked a few bottles while no-one was looking.'

West checked her watch.

'Interview terminated,' she said, glancing at Bowen as she stood. 'The time is four thirty-two pm. I'm sorry. I'm just doing my job.'

'Aye. And you're keeping me from doing mine. So, let's have it. Are you locking me up or letting me go? I need to ring Ally.'

'I'll let you know.'

* * *

Berating herself for blowing her chances with the motorcycling medic, and determined not to make the same mistake with him as she'd made with Mary Ferguson, West concluded that, Buprenorphine aside, all the available evidence simply substantiated Bowen's version of events leaving her no choice but to gamble on him being innocent.

'Dougal,' she said as she stomped into the office clutching Bowen's phone, 'check this would you, I can't be arsed.'

'What am I looking for, miss?'

'The night Jardine snuffed it, he says he called for an ambulance.'

'Aye, right enough,' said Dougal. 'It's all here. Nine, nine, nine. The call lasted two minutes and seventeen seconds.'

'And before that?'

'Somebody called Ally.'

Munro, sensing she'd been bolting after Bowen like a belligerent bloodhound with a blocked nose, glanced up from his newspaper and removed his spectacles.

'Looks to me like you've been thrown off the scent, lassie.'

West tousled her hair and groaned.

'He had all the right answers, Jimbo,' she said forlornly. 'He was the one who found Jardine, and he was the one who rang for an ambulance, and he even admits to losing his bleeding glove while he was making the call. I hate to say it, but we should be thanking him, really.'

'And what about the 'prenorphine?'

'It's not that easy to come by. Apparently. And frankly, if he had got hold of some, I wouldn't be surprised if he used it on himself. And to top it all, we've got bugger all to link him to Byrne.'

'Except for the loan.'

'But that's just it,' said West. 'It's the loan. Not his death.'

'So, what's next?' said Duncan. 'Will we see if any of that 'prenorphine's gone missing from the hospital?'

'No. Take his phone, give it back, and tell him he's free to go.'

'So, we're not charging him?'

'With what?' said West, reaching for her coat. 'Being a fine, upstanding citizen with his daughter's best interests at heart?'

'That'll be a no, then.'

'I'm off, I've got some serious thinking to do, and I suggest you two do the same. Go get a pint, you've earned it.'

'Not yet, miss,' said Dougal, 'it's just the back of five, we'll have a chat with Foubert before we go.'

'Okay, good call.'

'The thing is, we'll need to get a statement off your registrar pal about his involvement with Foubert, is that okay?'

'No skin off my nose,' said West. 'You should do the same with anyone who's dealt with him. Did you contact HMRC?'

'Aye, we should get copies of his tax returns tomorrow.'

'Good, as soon as you've got that, you can charge him. Hit him with everything you've got.'

Chapter 17

Compared to working with officers who regarded her as nothing more than a statistic on the equal opportunities programme while they wandered the seedier side of Shoreditch hunting for villains whose criminal prowess was limited to stealing bicycles, coping with a crippling case of self-doubt over the culpability of her main suspect was – with the freedom to think for herself and answer to no-one but the DCI – a walk in the park.

With a Balvenie in hand and the laptop by her side, West sat cross-legged on the sofa trying to make sense of the list of names she'd scribbled on the notepad, each linked by an almost indecipherable array of arrows connecting Craig Ferguson to his wife, Macallan and Jardine; Jardine to Macallan and Byrne; Byrne to Bowen and Foubert; and Foubert to Jardine and Bowen, while Munro, keeping an eye on what was left of the whisky, pulverised a pan of potatoes into a mountain of creamy mash.

'Are you getting anywhere, Charlie?'

'I certainly am,' said West. 'It's a place called nowhere. Population: one.'

'At least you'll not be troubled by noisy neighbours.'

West put down her pen, cradled the glass in both hands, and stared at Munro.

'You know what?' she said. 'I'm seriously thinking I should have turned down the promotion. It's not going to do me any favours when I draw a blank over this one.'

'Nonsense, lassie. It's your first case as an SIO, you'll get there eventually.'

'Not at this rate, I won't. The more I look at it, the more frustrated I become. Maybe I'm not cut out for this after all.'

'Now, you listen to me, lassie. You didnae get the post as DI on a whim, nobody was doing you a favour. You got there on merit, but if you're going to roll over because you cannae solve one simple conundrum, then perhaps you're right. Maybe you should just pack your bags and head back to London.'

'You know something?' said West, smirking as she drained her glass. 'If you were my dad...'

'Careful now.'

'...I'd have left home ages ago.'

'And you'd have come running back before you reached the end of the street.'

'What makes you so sure?'

'Because,' said Munro as he placed the plates on the table, 'nobody in their right mind would walk away from a supper like this.'

West leapt from the sofa like a voracious cur and eyed the burnt offering with a playful glint in her eye.

'Correct me if I'm wrong,' she said, reaching for the gravy, 'but did they use to be lamb chops?'

'Black is the new pink, lassie. I thought you knew that. So, come on, what's the problem?'

'Oh, I don't know,' said West. 'Mental block, I suppose. No matter how I look at it, I keep coming back to Mary Ferguson but there's nothing to prove it.'

'Unlike Bowen.'

'Yeah, but he couldn't have done it, there's no way he could've got his hands on the 'prenorphine.'

'Och, you know your trouble, Charlie? You're too trusting. The man's a doctor, he works in the hospital. If he'd wanted to, he could have got hold of the stuff, nae bother.'

West reached for her phone, dialled a number, and set it on the table.

'Sorry, Jimbo,' she said as they waited for a response, 'but I think you're way off there. Don't get me wrong, I'm not doing this to prove you're wrong, I'm doing it for my own peace of mind.'

'McLeod.'

'Andy. It's DI West, I hope I'm not disturbing you.'

'No, you're alright. How can I help?'

'Quick question,' said West. 'Buprenorphine.'

'Oh, aye. Is this to do with the fella in the car park?'

'Yes, it is. Listen, I'm just wondering, hypothetically speaking, say you worked in a hospital and you wanted to get your hands on some 'prenorphine, how easy would that be? I mean, if it wasn't used in your department?'

'Easy.'

'No, no,' said West, 'I don't mean, officially. I mean, if you wanted some for, let's say, personal use?'

'I'll say it again, Inspector. Easy.'

West glanced at Munro, her appetite suddenly on the wane.

'What? But how?' she said. 'I thought all medication was kept under lock and key?'

'Right enough,' said McLeod, 'but it's not Fort Knox, Inspector. Access to medication is restricted, of course, and the use of anything like Buprenorphine would have to be entered on the Controlled Drugs Register, but just like anything else, if you can avoid detection, then anyone could steal it.'

'But it must be risky, surely? I mean, with CCTV and stuff, no-one would be that stupid, would they?'

'Here's the thing,' said McLeod, 'stuff goes missing every day and the NHS take it very seriously, but the bottom line is, they're more concerned with the financial loss rather than who took it and nine times out of ten, any shortfall is listed as a stock discrepancy.'

'So, what you're saying is, if you wanted it, you could get it?'

'Without a doubt.'

'I see,' said West as she hung up. 'Thanks.'

Munro mopped his plate with a slice of bread and butter and sat back with satisfied sigh.

'Two words,' he said. 'Cat. Pigeons.'

'You're a great help.'

'It doesnae mean he did it, Charlie. It means he could have, if he'd wanted to.'

'Two more words,' said West. 'Square, and one.'

Munro slid the plate to one side and topped up their glasses.

'Remember what I said to Rona Macallan, Charlie? About leaving no stone unturned?'

'Yeah, what of it?'

'You've one more to flip, lassie. You've one more to flip.'

* * *

As someone who'd made a concerted effort to confine the shock of the unexpected to his professional career, Munro had come to rely upon routine as a way of maintaining his equilibrium but with compromise and concessions being the bywords of a house guest he was finding it difficult to keep his balance, particularly when greeted by the sight of a dishevelled DI with eyes as black as frying pans hunched over the dining table at six-fifteen in the morning.

'Jumping Jehoshaphat!' he said. 'Is it not a bit early for Halloween?'

'Sorry?' said West, peering over the laptop.

'You, lassie! You look terrible.'

'Thanks very much.'

'Did you not sleep?'

'Not much.'

'What on earth have you been doing all night?'

'Flipping stones,' said West as she stretched and stood. 'Like pancakes.'

'This is getting to be a habit, Charlie, and it doesnae suit you. I'll make some coffee.'

'Ta. I'll grab a quick shower then we can get going.'

'Going?' said Munro. 'Going where? I've not had my porridge, yet.'

'I'll buy you breakfast,' said West. 'Anything you like, the full works.'

'You've still not said, Charlie. Where are we going?'

'If I'm right,' said West, 'somewhere that'll prove I've stopped thinking like a normal person.'

'And if you're wrong?'

'Doesn't bear thinking about, Jimbo. Stick the kettle on.'

* * *

Refusing to travel in the cramped conditions of the pint-sized Figaro, Munro – left with no alternative but to act as chauffeur – swung the Peugeot onto the forecourt, killed the engine, and smiled knowingly as he glanced towards the veterinary clinic.

'You took your time, Charlie,' he said. 'Let's just hope it was worth the wait.'

'Amen to that,' said West as she drew a deep breath, 'but I'm not out of the woods yet. Are you coming in?'

'No, no. This is your shout. On you go.'

* * *

Unable to locate a bell, a knocker, or even a letterbox, and with well over an hour to go before they opened for business, West resorted to a tried and tested technique for eliciting a response and began battering the door with the side of her fist until the sound of the bolts being drawn from the inside prompted her to take a step back.

An annoyingly fresh-faced blonde girl wearing a crisp, white tunic opened the door and smiled.

'Hello,' she said, her disposition far too cheery for such an early hour. 'Is it an emergency?'

'You could say that. I'm looking for somebody called Colin.'

'You mean Mr McCarthy? Come inside and I'll fetch him for you. Is he in the car? Your pet?'

West, unable to contain herself, sniggered under her breath.

'He is, yes.'

'Poor wee thing. And what do you have?'

'He's a Rottweiler.'

'Okay, very good,' said the girl as she buzzed the consulting room, 'and what seems to be the problem?'

'Nothing,' said West as she flashed her warrant card, 'he's as fit as a fiddle. I need to talk to Colin about something else.'

'That'll be me, you're after,' said McCarthy, 'you'd best come in.'

* * *

Compared to others in the medical profession she'd had cause to work with or interview – in particular pathologists and registrars – the bespectacled Colin McCarthy, at a little over five feet tall with hair like a bird's nest and a prominent pot-belly, fell short of expectations.

'DI West,' she said. 'Can I have a word?'

McCarthy hoisted himself onto a stool and sat with his hands dangling between his knees.

'I must say, this is a first for us,' he said. 'I can't remember ever having a visit from the police before.'

'Well, you can relax,' said West. 'It's not you I've come about.'

'That's a relief. I think. Oh, it's not one of my staff, is it?'

'No. It's about a friend of yours; Miss Rona Macallan?'

West, intrigued by McCarthy's shifty sideways glance and the way he impulsively cleared his throat, shoved her hands in her pockets and leaned against the wall as he jumped from the stool, overwhelmed by a sudden compulsion to tidy the counter behind him.

'Rona!' he said. 'Dear Rona. What exactly do you need to know?'

West remained silent until McCarthy, feeling the burn of her stare on the back of his head, finally turned around.

'How long have you two been seeing each other?' she said with a wry smile.

'I don't know what you mean.'

'It's alright, Mr McCarthy, you don't have to answer. It's none of my business.'

'A while,' said McCarthy. 'A long while.'

'Okay,' said West. 'Happy?'

'Very.'

'Good. Now the real reason I'm here is to ask you about the Vetergesic.'

'Oh, aye?'

'She said you gave her some.'

'I did indeed. That's not an offence, is it?'

'I really don't know,' said West. 'I'd have to look into it. Maybe. If it wasn't used to treat colic.'

'That couldn't happen, Inspector. Rona's been around animals her entire life, she's very careful and I trust her implicitly. She's more than capable of administering a dose.'

'I don't doubt it for a minute,' said West, 'but let's get down to the nitty-gritty. She says you gave her just the right amount for a few jabs, is that right?'

'It is, aye.'

'A couple of syringes? Ready to go?'

'No, no,' said McCarthy, shaking his head, 'that wouldn't even touch the sides, besides, much as I love Rona, I'm a busy man, I don't have time to go loading syringes with the correct dose, especially for someone who knows what they're doing.'

'So, what did you give her?

'Why, four bottles, of course. Ten millilitres each.'

West, hiding her delight, walked towards the door.

'Just out of interest,' she said, 'if that was given to someone by mistake…

'You mean a human?'

'Yeah, say twenty, thirty mils, what would…?'

'Oh, not good, Inspector. Dearie me, no. Not good at all.'

Chapter 18

With her confidence boosted to unprecedented levels, West – feeling as high as a hippy with a pipeful of hash – crashed back to earth as they approached Macallan's house and pulled into the empty drive.

'It's gone!' she said, excitedly. 'Jimbo! The Defender. It's gone!'

'Calm yourself, lassie. She's probably away up the shops.'

'Shops my arse!' said West as she leapt from the car. 'She's done a bleeding runner!'

Unfazed by her panicked reaction, Munro unfastened his safety belt and glanced towards the field before reclining his seat, lying back and closing his eyes while she took a quick look around.

'There's no answer,' she said as she flung open the door, 'I'm going to… what the hell are you doing?'

'I'm having a cat-nap,' said Munro, 'although, I do believe folk nowadays refer to it as a power nap. Whichever way you look at it, though, it's still forty winks.'

'Are you insane? You're just going to lie there while she's halfway to…'

'She's not halfway to anywhere, Charlie. You're reverting to form and jumping to conclusions.'

'Am I indeed? The house is locked up, the car's gone…'

'And the ponies are in the paddock, the chickens are in the run, and the goats are chewing the cud. She'll not be far. Trust me.'

West slumped in her seat and sighed.

'I hope you're right,' she said, 'or my future's up the Swanee.'

'It's not the future you should be scared of, Charlie. It's repeating the past.'

West glanced at Munro and rolled her eyes.

'Thanks, Sigmund,' she said. 'That's really cheered me up.'

'Is Duncan on his way?'

'Yeah, shouldn't be long. So, what do we do now?'

'What do you think?' said Munro as he began to doze. 'We wait.'

* * *

Unable to relax as West rummaged through the glove box rustling wrappers like a ravenous rat in search of something to eat, Munro opened his eyes, returned his seat to the upright position, and cocked his head at the sound of a vehicle speeding up the lane.

'Duncan,' he said as the Audi pulled up behind them.

'Alright, chief? Miss? You said it was urgent, what's occurring?'

'Macallan,' said West. 'We're bringing her in.'

'Magic. Where is she?'

'She'll not be long,' said Munro. 'Listen, park on the road will you, and when she arrives, I want you to box her in. Just in case.'

'Roger that, chief.'

Munro turned to West as Duncan reversed down the drive.

'Remember your offer of breakfast, Charlie?'

'Yup. What about it?'

'It's accruing interest, it'll be lunch now.'

'Play your cards right and it might be the last supper. Here we go.'

West stepped from the car as Rona, waving and grinning like a long lost relative at a family reunion, parked alongside.

'You should've called,' she said. 'I'd have waited in for you.'

'Impulse,' said Munro, 'makes life a wee bit more exciting, wouldn't you say?'

'Aye, I would that, Mr Munro. Come away inside, it's getting chilly.'

* * *

Macallan grabbed three mugs from the sideboard, took a pot of coffee from the hob, and joined Munro and West at the table.

'Milk, Mr Munro?'

'Aye, thanking you. Although, no. On second thought, I think I'll take it black.'

'How have you been?' said West.

'Oh, fine. The usual routine, but I'm sleeping better knowing a nutter's not going to knock on my door.'

'How d'you mean?'

'That Jardine fella,' said Macallan. 'Did you not say he was dead?'

'Aye, we did,' said Munro. 'But apart from that, you've nothing new to report? No other trouble?'

'No, no. Life goes on.'

'For some, Miss Macallan. For some. Speaking of which, have you seen young Craig recently?'

'I have, indeed. He's looking much better but I'm not sure if that's to do with the rose quartz I took for under his pillow, or the cheese.'

'My money's on the cheese,' said West, smiling glibly. 'Calcium.'

Munro sipped his coffee, grimaced at the bitter taste, and reached for the sugar pot.

'Tell me,' he said, tipping three spoonfuls into his mug, 'what do you do about your animals, Miss Macallan, when you go away? I mean, they cannae fend for themselves, do you have someone to look after them?'

'I do, aye. The fella over the way. He's good like that.'

'You might want to give him a call.'

'I already have.'

'Come again?' said West.

'I've been expecting you,' said Macallan. 'I had a call this morning. From Colin.'

'I see. I must say, you don't seem very…'

'Upset? Why would I be?'

'For obvious reasons, I'd have thought.'

'No, no,' said Macallan. 'See here, Inspector, I know I've done wrong, something terrible in fact, but I had my reasons and I'll take the consequences, whatever they are.'

'If there were more like you,' said Munro, 'I'm not sure the legal profession would have a need for lawyers.'

Macallan smiled as she stood and reached for the cupboard under the sink.

'I've something for you,' she said, placing a small, brown box on the table. 'The Vetergesic. I thought you might be needing it.'

'Are you having a laugh?' said West. 'I mean, most people would've tried to bin the evidence.'

'Most people,' said Macallan, 'but not me. I believe in honesty, Inspector. I'll not be haunted by the repercussions of lying.'

West leaned back, crossed her arms and regarded Macallan with an inquisitive frown.

'Why?' she said. 'Why did you kill Alan Byrne and Sean Jardine?'

'Oh, I didn't kill them,' said Macallan. 'I euthanised them.'

'You what?'

'They weren't comfortable in their own skins…'

'Well, they aren't now.'

'…they had issues. I sent them to a better place.'

'Did you, by George?' said Munro, huffing with surprise. 'I'm not sure they'd agree with that.'

'And the beads around their wrists,' said West, 'I'm assuming you gave them to Mark as a finishing touch?'

'I did, aye.'

'Well, I've seen some things in my time, Miss Macallan,' said Munro, 'but a vigilante Buddhist? That's a first.'

'It's a pity, really,' said West, 'if you'd had known from the off that this was all over fifty quid, it might never have happened.'

'Right enough. But there's no going back, now, is there?'

'It still doesn't explain why.'

Munro watched as Macallan, toying with the ring on her finger, stared into her mug and smiled wistfully to herself.

'Craig,' she said. 'He needed protecting, looking after. He's a vulnerable lad.'

'Go on.'

'Did you know that he'd been set upon before? Twice in fact. Just for being gay. And when Byrne… well, it's bullying, plain and simple, and I'll not tolerate bullying.'

'You're to be commended on that score,' said Munro, 'but you cannae go taking the law into your own hands.'

'I'm aware of that Mr Munro, but what was the alternative? Sit back and watch Craig take another beating? Or go to the police who'd have probably laughed and told him to man-up?'

'And what about Jardine?' said West. 'How did you know about his involvement?'

'Byrne mentioned his name. He said if I ever changed my mind about things and I couldn't get hold of him, then I was to contact Jardine instead. After what happened to Craig and Byrne already dead, I knew he had to be behind it. You can see I had no choice.'

'We always have a choice, Miss Macallan,' said Munro. 'That's what separates us from the animals in the zoo.'

'Aye. Right enough. So, what happens now?'

'Well, we're going to arrest you for murder. Then, we'll take you to the station where you'll be charged, and tomorrow you'll be in court.'

'Right-oh. And is that me away for life, then?'

'We'll let the judge decide, shall we?' said West. 'On the plus side, as you've admitted the offence, I doubt it'll be trial by jury, so a few words from us about your co-operation and the judge might show some leniency.'

'So, not life?'

'Miss Macallan,' said Munro, 'we clearly cannae comment, you understand?'

'Aye, sorry.'

'But, if you get yourself a good brief, he might be able to argue self-defence or justifiable homicide as far as Jardine's concerned.'

'And Byrne?'

'Who knows? Bearing in mind the course of events leading up to his death, diminished responsibility might be a feasible plea.'

'And what will happen to my house?' said Macallan.

'It'll be here when you get out,' said Munro, 'but I'd advise you to get someone to look after it. A lodger, perhaps.'

'The car'll not be up to much, though, will it?'

'Probably not.'

'Do you not see yourself in a Defender, Mr Munro?' said Macallan. 'Or you, Inspector?'

'Well, actually,' said West, 'I was thinking of…'

'We'll have to check protocol on that,' said Munro, interrupting. 'I'm not sure it's the done thing.'

'Right you are,' said Macallan. 'Well, it's there for the taking if you want it. So, is that us away, then?'

'Aye,' said Munro. 'It is. DC Reid's outside, he'll give you a lift, make sure you get checked-in alright, and escort you to your room.'

Chapter 19

Confounded by Munro's apparent lack of enthusiasm for the apprehension of Rona Macallan, and unsettled by the increasingly uncomfortable silence as they trundled their way back to the office, West, assuming she was somehow to blame for his sullen mood, finally snapped.

'Look,' she said, 'if you're in a strop just because we haven't eaten yet, it's not my fault, alright?'

Munro cast her a sideways glance and smiled.

'It's not that, lassie,' he said, 'but as you've broached the subject then you should know that as we're fast approaching suppertime I'm in mind of a T-bone with apple pie and custard for pudding.'

'So, what's up then? Why the long face?'

'Something's not right.'

'Not right?' said West. 'Are you kidding? It's just been handed to us on a plate.'

'Exactly.'

'I don't get it.'

'Why would she keep the bottles?'

'She told you why. To make reparations for her sins.'

'No, no,' said Munro. 'That's not it. She's leading us on, Charlie, I'm sure of it. It's almost as if she wanted to be caught.'

'Well, of course she did!' said West. 'She's riddled with guilt, but I agree, it is slightly odd, and that's why I'm going to recommend her for a psychiatric assessment when we get back.'

'Is that so?'

'Yup, let's face it, Jimbo, she's clearly off her trolley. Barking. A crust short of a loaf. Besides, if they do find she's a bit... unbalanced, they'll give her an easy ride. She'll be holed-up in a cushy wing instead of a maximum security number. The worst that could happen is that they'll pump her full of Olanzapine but at least she'll be out in a few years.'

'Right enough,' said Munro, unconvinced. 'So, what got you there, Charlie? Which stone did you flip?'

'The same one Bowen was hiding under.'

'Go on.'

'Frankly, I was stupid,' said West, 'I double-checked his story about getting hold of the 'prenorphine, didn't I? Alright, I admit it was just to prove a point to you and as is it turned out, I was wrong, but I hadn't done that with Macallan. I hadn't spoken to the vet to verify what she'd said was true.'

'And that's what's bugging me, Charlie.'

'What is?'

'Why did she lie about the 'prenorphine she got from the vet when she's normally so keen on telling the truth?'

'Stop worrying,' said West as she threw head back and sighed. 'There's bound to be a reason. It'll come to me. Eventually.'

* * *

After a rewarding one-to-one with Claude Foubert in the privacy of the interview room, Dougal – confident of a successful prosecution for tax evasion, illegal money lending, and harassment – finalised the paperwork for the procurator fiscal while Duncan, sensing congratulations were in order, gave the pot a stir and laid out a selection of biscuits in anticipation of West's return.

'Nice going on your first collar as the SIO, miss,' he said. 'We're made up for you.'

'Aye, we are indeed,' said Dougal. 'Well done.'

'We're not there yet,' said West as she slung her coat over a chair, 'but thanks, anyway.'

'Shame really,' said Duncan, 'she's alright, that Rona Macallan. Nice lady, wouldn't stop gassing all the way back.'

'Is that so?'

'Oh, aye. Good looking, too. In fact, if I wasn't with Cathy I might be tempted to…'

'That's quite enough of that, thank you,' said West with a smirk. 'Right, we've still got work to do. Where is she?'

'Downstairs, miss. Ready when you are but we thought you might like a celebration brew first, complete with chocolate wafers.'

'That's what I like about you, Duncan. You get your priorities right, but first I need these bagged and dusted, please.'

'Right away,' said Dougal as she handed him the cardboard box. 'Are you okay, boss? You're not saying much?'

Munro, hands clasped behind his back, gave him a half-hearted smile and walked to the window as West, tired of his sulking, rolled her eyes and took a biscuit from the plate.

'Miss,' said Dougal as he inspected the bottles before sealing them in a plastic pouch, 'did you get these from Macallan?'

'Yup. It's the stuff she used to polish off Byrne and Jardine.'

'Did you not look in the box when she gave it to you?'

'No need,' said West, 'it's just a bunch of empty bottles.'

'Not quite, miss. In fact, if you're thinking of submitting these as evidence, then you've got a wee problem on your hands.'

'What do you mean?'

'They're not empty. They've not even been opened. The seals are still intact.'

West, looking as shell-shocked as a Tommy in the trenches, glanced first at Duncan and then at Dougal before locking eyes with Munro.

'What's she playing at?' she said, her brow as furrowed as a freshly ploughed field.

'Oh, she probably gave you the wrong box,' said Duncan. 'Perhaps there's another one with...'

'It's not the wrong box, you balloon!' said Munro. 'She cannae stockpile the stuff like aspirin, laddie!'

'Okay, hang on,' said West, 'let's rewind a bit, all this bickering is getting us nowhere. So, she gave me the box because she wanted to get caught, right? The question is, why?'

Duncan stared at the ceiling and scraped the stubble on his chin.

'Go it!' he said in a flash of inspiration. 'She suffers with Angel of Mercy syndrome! She kills these fellas but all the while she was hoping...'

'No, no, no,' said Munro. 'Folk who have that disorder want to get caught, I'll give you that, but nine times out of ten they want to get caught *in the act*. They want to be seen trying to save their victim. The fact of the matter is, Rona Macallan didnae want to be caught at all...'

'What?'

'...but when she was, she wanted to be arrested and she wanted to be found guilty. That's your "why".'

'But that's bonkers,' said West. 'Who in their right mind...'

'You've already said, Charlie. You dinnae think she is in her right mind.'

'Unless,' said Dougal. 'No, you're alright. It's too far-fetched.'

'No, go on,' said West. 'Let's hear it.'

'Unless… she was covering for somebody else.'

'You're right, it's too far-fetched.'

'Perhaps it's one for the psychiatrist, then,' said Munro, still fixated by the view from the window. 'Perhaps you should give him a ring.'

'I don't have his number.'

Munro slowly turned, zipped his coat and glared at West, his ice-blue eyes drilling into her head.

'Perhaps,' he said, 'you should give him… *a ring.*'

West, feeling as though she could do with a spell on the couch alongside Macallan, stared at Dougal as Munro slipped silently from the room, her eyes widening as the penny dropped.

'Holy crap!' she said, her voice as soft as a whisper. 'She's married! Rona Macallan's bleeding-well married! She's wearing a ring, third finger, left hand!'

'I'm on it, miss,' said Dougal as his fingers flew across the keyboard. 'Just give me a minute.'

* * *

Unlike the majority of detainees who insisted on protesting their innocence by maintaining a smug silence or flying into a defensive rage, Rona Macallan, despite the ice-cold glare of an irate West, remained as cool as the proverbial cucumber.

Sitting cross-legged in the stark surroundings of the interview room, she smiled as West pulled up a chair whilst Munro, choosing to stand, remained by the door.

'This won't take long,' said West. 'There's just a couple of things we need to clear up.'

'No bother,' said Macallan. 'If I can help, I will.'

'First of all, you should know we're dropping the murder charge.'

'Dropping it? What do you mean?'

'I mean you will now be charged with perverting the course of justice.'

'I don't understand.'

West leaned back, folded her arms and glowered across the desk at Macallan.

'Nice ring,' she said, nodding towards her left hand.

'Sorry?'

'Your ring. Gold, is it?'

'Oh, this old thing?' said Macallan, raising her hand. 'It is, indeed. It's only nine carat but it's not bad, is it?'

'Do you wear it for a reason?'

'Aye, it's the oldest trick in the book. It keeps the neds at bay, you know, the chancers who think they might be in with a shout.'

'I see. So, you're not married then?'

'Married?' said Macallan, laughing softly as she shook her head. 'No, no. I'm not the marrying kind, me.'

'So, you've no recollection of ever going to Saint Margaret's? The church on John Street?'

Macallan glanced furtively at Munro, her smile wavering.

'I'm not one for religion.'

'Well, in that case I'm obviously wasting my time,' said West, 'because you definitely won't remember walking down the aisle…'

'Aisle?'

'…and exchanging vows with a certain Mark Alisdair Bowen.'

Macallan pursed her lips and sighed as Munro, reaching into his coat pocket, stepped forward and placed a small, blue, polished stone on the desk in front her.

'Sodalite,' said Macallan. 'Very good, Mr Munro. Very good, indeed.'

'Let's start again, shall we?' said West. 'Why were you covering for your husband? Your estranged husband?'

Macallan bowed her head.

'Ally,' she said. 'I did it for Ally.'

'She's your daughter?'

'She is.'

'Go on.'

Macallan took a deep breath, raised her head and regarded West with a look of defeat.

'Mark was struggling,' she said. 'Physically, mentally, and financially. He came to me not long after he'd got this loan, a big loan, from Alan Byrne. He thought not having to worry about money would ease the pressure but Byrne started getting heavy.'

'Why?' said West. 'Was he missing the repayments?'

'No. Quite the opposite. See here, Inspector, crooks like that never want the loan paid off, that's how they work. They keep folk forever in their debt. Mark was paying back extra but Byrne kept raising the interest rate. Then, he showed up at work a couple of times, with Sean Jardine.'

'So, your husband knew Jardine?'

'He did, aye. They started threatening him, they even said they'd torch the house while Ally was in her bed.'

'Well, why didn't you go to the police about it?'

'Come now, Inspector, and say what? There's no paper trail, no official agreement. And if we did, what would happen if Byrne and Jardine got wind of it? They'd have set about him and left him in a worse state than Craig.'

'So, what happened next?'

'What do you think?' said Macallan. 'We decided to do something about it.'

'Kill them?'

'Get them off his back. We talked about it long and hard, the last thing either of us wanted was for anything to happen to Ally.'

'And?'

'Mark knows I wouldn't lift a finger to a fly, so he said that he'd take care of it; but I said we had to do it properly, cover his tracks, so if anyone came calling, like yourselves, he'd not get done for it.'

'And that's why,' said West, 'you agreed to take the fall for him?'

'Aye.'

'But why?'

'Guilt, I suppose,' said Macallan. 'It's my fault he got himself into this mess. I walked out on them, for no other reason than marrying too young, I suppose. I left them struggling and Mark... well, I owed him big time. I never realised at the time but he'd got himself heavily into debt because he'd helped me out, setting up here with all the livestock and such.'

'And Ally knows nothing about it?'

'She does not. She has enough to deal with, she doesn't deserve to bear the burden of our worries, not at her age.'

'That's all very well,' said West, 'but surely if we'd nicked your husband then she could've stayed with you.'

'In theory, perhaps, but not practically. See, despite the debts, Mark still earns ten times more than I do, and he's got the house. There's no way I could support myself and Ally, not with her away to university. So we agreed, if he took care of the problem and I got caught, then it wouldn't be so bad. I'd be away for a few years and that would be that.'

'Wouldn't Ally get suspicious if you just disappeared off the radar?'

'We rarely see each other. That's how good a mother I am.'

'And is she aware of what's going on?' said West. 'With the loan?'

'She is. Mark keeps nothing from her, and she'll not leave his side at the moment. If he's working nights, she'll stop at a friend's house.'

'Okay,' said West, 'so if your husband took care of Byrne and Jardine, where did he get the Buprenorphine from?'

'The hospital, I imagine.'

'And with those two out of the way, you thought it was all over but you didn't count on Claude Foubert popping up, did you?'

'You got to him before us.'

'And if we hadn't?'

Macallan raised her eyebrows and smiled.

'You could have got away with it,' said West. 'If you'd remembered to empty the bottles of Vetergesic, you could have got away with it.'

'I know,' said Macallan. 'I realised my mistake as soon as I handed you the box. It was the weight, you see, but I couldn't very well ask for it back, now, could I? It was a silly mistake and now I've made things worse.'

'Yup. I have to agree with you there,' said West. 'A lot worse. Still, at least Ally will have a roof over her head and she won't have to worry about money or fees.'

'So, she'll be okay?'

'Probably not. I reckon she'll be psychologically scarred for life.'

Munro took four steps forward and stopped alongside Macallan.

'Your pony,' he said, addressing the back wall, 'did he have colic?'

'No. He was fine, Mr Munro. Just fine. So, what happens now? Are you away to arrest Mark?'

'We are,' said West.

'And me?'

'And you? Rona Macallan, I'm charging you with perverting the course of justice and aiding and abetting Mr

197

Mark Bowen in the murders of Alan Byrne and Sean Jardine. Do you understand the charge?'

Macallan smiled and nodded.

'I do. Aye.'

'Is there anything you'd like to say in reply to the charge?'

'Guilty. Guilty as hell.'

* * *

Engrossed in the most rewarding internet search he'd ever attempted, Dougal – looking as pleased as punch – sat grinning at the screen whilst Duncan, lounging with his feet up on the desk, devoured the remaining biscuits as he made arrangements for a quiet night in.

'So, any plans, Dougal?' he said. 'Are you not having a rematch with that Emily girl?'

'I am. We're having pizza.'

'Good call. No offence but that way, if she gets hammered, you'll not be stuck with her, you can ship her off in a taxi. Where are you headed?'

'My place.'

'Oh.'

'No, it's fine,' said Dougal. 'See here, I've just discovered you can get wine that's alcohol-free. I'm going to pick some up on the way home, that way if she feels the urge, she'll not get blootered.'

'Covering all the bases, eh? Good for you, although I can't see the point myself. It's like having coffee without the caffeine.'

'How about you?' said Dougal. 'Are you off out?'

'No, no,' said Duncan. 'I'm driving over to Cathy's for a quiet night in – a pile of poppadums and a vindaloo. Magic. So, what do you reckon to Westy and this Bowen fella, do you think she's nailed it?'

'Oh, aye. On the head. I just hope Macallan's telling her what she needs to know so we don't have to drag it out of her.'

'Drag what out of who?' said West, beaming as she breezed through the door.

'Macallan, miss. We were just saying…'

'She has. She told us everything and I have to say, I can't help feeling sorry for her.'

'How so?' said Dougal.

'Because they were just trying to get by, but what makes it worse is it's not as if they wanted the money for betting, booze or fags, they simply wanted it to get their daughter through uni.'

'Right enough.'

'And I can't blame Bowen for wanting some breathing space. A holiday, even.'

'So, what now?'

'Now, you have the privilege of arresting him. I want the two of you to shoot over to the hospital and pick him up…'

'Roger that,' said Duncan.

'…and as soon as you've booked him in, we're all off for a night out. I'm paying.'

Dougal, not wanting to let the side down, glanced at Duncan before speaking.

'The thing is, miss,' he said, sheepishly, 'I'm supposed to be meeting Emily but I can cancel, no bother. I'll just give her a wee call and tell her…'

'You'll do no such thing,' said West. 'Let's hope she stays upright this time. How about you, Duncan? Are you bailing out, too?'

'Cathy,' said Duncan with a nod. 'Sorry, but we're all set.'

'Well, it looks like it's you and me again, Jimbo. Unless, of course…'

'No, no,' said Munro, 'you're not getting off the hook that easily, lassie. I've fasted all day and I need to pile on the beef. You should know, I'm having a starter, too.'

Epilogue

Compensated by the calming influence of a flavoursome, full-bodied red and the view from the table which offered the enchanting spectacle of a solitary cargo ship bobbing across the moonlit estuary as it made its way to port, Munro was willing to overlook the inefficiency of the kitchen and forgive the brusque manner of the harangued staff as he waited patiently for his meal to arrive.

'When I said I fancied a starter, Charlie, I was thinking of a bowl of soup or some pâté and toast, not a packet of dry roasted peanuts.'

'Well, I offered you some goats' cheese but you didn't want it,' said West as she plonked the plates on the table. 'Here you go. This is better than sitting in some stuffy restaurant, isn't it?'

'Aye, right enough,' said Munro as he ripped through his steak. 'I must admit, the last thing I want just now is some waiter hovering over my shoulder with a poker up his arse.'

'Exactly. I mean, what more could you want? A twelve-ounce sirloin cremated just the way you like it. Cheers.'

'Your very good health,' said Munro. 'So, tell me honestly now, are you happy with the result?'

'Well, I have to say, it's not bad,' said West, 'although I think I'd have preferred mine not so well-done.'

'By jiminy! I'm talking about the case, Charlie, not the fodder!'

'Oh, that. Yeah, couldn't be better. As they used to say down south – a right result.'

'So, I take it this means you'll not be packing your bags, then?'

'Will I heck,' said West. 'I'm staying put and mark my words, next time, there'll be no false starts.'

'I'm glad to hear. Now, two things before I forget.'

'Oh, God. Here we go. What is it now?'

'Have you any plans for tomorrow?'

'Well, I've got to interview Bowen again, then charge him, then sort out the paperwork, but unless anything else comes up, I should be done by late afternoon. Why?'

'I thought you might like to see Auchencairn,' said Munro.

'Ork and who?'

'It's a wee village.'

'What's there?'

'Not much, really. A shop and a post office. A castle. And a pub that shut down a couple of years back.'

'Sounds riveting.'

'Oh, and there's a wee cottage for sale. Three beds and a garden big enough to turn your fingers green.'

'I'm in,' said West. 'What was the other thing?'

'The apple pie. Is it in the oven?'

* * *

Unaware of her mother's impending internment or her father's imminent re-arrest, a shattered and somewhat distraught Alison Bowen – exhausted from the two and a half hour train journey from Ayr to Edinburgh followed by a further two on the connecting service to Durham, with nothing to eat but a Big Mac and a soggy serving of French fries – grabbed her phone and sent her father a reassuring text advising him of her safe arrival as her fellow passengers gathered their belongings and congregated by the door.

With well over a year to go until her studies were complete, and with an evening shift in a nearby pub providing her only source of income, she sighed with indecision as she contemplated quitting her course for the umpteenth time if only to rid herself of the guilt of being the cause of her parent's unassailable debt.

Despite his good looks and obvious wealth – apparent from the watch on his wrist and the spanking new Range Rover – Alan Byrne, she'd conceded, was neither brash nor ostentatious but a polite, softly-spoken Englishman with impeccable manners who instilled a sense of trust.

Once he'd explained, in an apologetic but matter-of-fact way that the loan he'd arranged was simply a business deal that her father was duty-bound to honour, she'd accepted the situation and was ready to walk away until he'd mentioned the "get-out" clause, an alternative arrangement which, should she be agreeable, would clear the debt in one fell swoop.

Had he not reneged on the deal, leaving her angry and annoyed for being so gullible, and had he not laughed in her face leaving her feeling sullied and used, then events may have taken a different turn.

Glancing over her shoulder as the hordes of commuters began to disembark, she hauled her rucksack from beneath the seat in front of her and, careful to avoid the prying eyes of the on-board CCTV, unzipped the side pocket, retrieved the spent vials of Buprenorphine and wrapped them in a paper napkin, placing them inside the empty burger box before burying it in the paper bag beneath the remnants of her meal and tossing it into the waste bin as she left the train.

Character List

JAMES MUNRO (RETIRED) – Unable to relinquish his duties as a DI, the irrepressible Munro finds a flaw in the rule book and adopts a volunteer role which lengthens his lifespan and puts his invaluable expertise to good use.

DI CHARLOTTE WEST – Dealing with her first case as a Senior Investigating Officer, "Charlie" is keen to make an impression and secure a swift result but after a couple of false starts it begins to look as though she have may have bitten off more than she can chew.

DS DOUGAL McCRAE – As a past master when it comes to approaching things from a sideways point of view, DS McCrae, normally unfazed by surprises, is caught on the hop when an unexpected invitation from an old flame leaves him floundering on the rocks.

DC DUNCAN REID – Keen to make amends for his hitherto maverick approach to policing, DC Reid takes the bull by the horns and soon starts to show his true worth.

DCI GEORGE ELLIOT – The ebullient DCI Elliot, stressed by staff cuts and under-funding, shows no hesitation when called upon to assist Munro in finding a way back into the force.

CRAIG FERGUSON – A clean-cut, software genius in the high-flying world of computer programming, Craig Ferguson appears to have it all, from a fancy flat to an attractive wife. Unfortunately for him, the only thing he doesn't have is happiness.

MARY FERGUSON – Unhappily married with a young child and an errant husband, recovering junkie Mary Ferguson is looking for a way out and she'll take the easiest route she can find.

RONA MACALLAN – As an animal-loving yoga fanatic Rona Macallan tends the livestock on her small-holding, eking out a meagre living by selling home-made organic produce but she hides a secret as dark as the barn on her farm.

SEAN JARDINE – A big man trapped in a small man's body, Sean Jardine, a wealthy investment banker, has anger-management issues which come to the fore when confronted by anyone he considers inferior to himself.

CLAUDE FOUBERT – A colleague of Jardine's, the sour-faced Frenchman has a talent for moving money around and making a substantial profit. Unfortunately, none of it belongs to the bank.

DR MARK BOWEN – Despite his role as Senior Registrar at the local Accident & Emergency department, Mark Bowen, struggling to put his daughter through university, is over-worked, underpaid and disappearing under a mountain of debt.

DR ANDY MCLEOD – More lumberjack than forensic pathologist, the hulking Andy McLeod is happiest in the company of a cadaver with no known cause of death.

If you enjoyed this book, please let others know by leaving a quick review on Amazon. Also, if you spot anything untoward in the paperback, get in touch. We strive for the best quality and appreciate reader feedback.

editor@thebookfolks.com

www.thebookfolks.com

Made in the USA
Lexington, KY
01 March 2019